CANARY
CHILD

David Field and Alan Dance

**ARUNDEL
BOOKS**

First published in Great Britain March 2014 by
Arundel Books, 2 Audon Avenue, Chilwell,
Nottingham NG9 4AW
www.arundelbooks.co.uk

This edition published August 2014

ISBN 978-0-9558133-6-8

Typeset in Plantin 11pt

Printed and bound in Great Britain by
CPI Antony Rowe Ltd., Chippenham, Wiltshire.

ACKNOWLEDGEMENTS

The authors wish to thank the following for their help and assistance in supplying historical information and details of the events of 1918 leading to the explosion at the Chilwell Shell Filling Factory, along with other historical and topographical information regarding the locations featured in this book, both in 1918 and 1968. Any errors which remain are entirely of our making.

Maureen Rushton, local historian and author of 'Canary Girls of Chilwell' (Beeston & District Local History Society, 2008).

Paula Hammond, for information about Attenborough and Attenborough Church.

Keith Reedman, Long Eaton local historian.

Val Bird, Chris Mellors and Frank Love for information about Bramcote.

Elaine Whiting for details of 1960s cuisine.

The staff at Long Eaton Library and Ilkeston Register Office.

Front cover image courtesy of the Imperial War Museums. © IWM Q30017. Photograph digitally cropped and tinted.

Rear cover from a photograph courtesy of Reg Baker and www.picturethepast.org.uk

"They shall grow not old, as we that are left grow old:
Age shall not weary them, nor the years condemn.
At the going down of the sun and in the morning
We will remember them."

Laurence Binyon
1869—1943

FOREWORD

Shortly after 7pm on 1st July 1918, a massive explosion blasted apart the shell-filling factory at Chilwell, some five miles west of Nottingham. The night shift had clocked on an hour earlier and had started their usual twelve-hour stint, filling with high explosive the shells which were turning the tide of the Great War in favour of the Allies in the trenches of Northern France.

To this day, little is known of what actually caused the explosion and there is still some doubt about precisely how many were killed. It was estimated that almost 140 perished in the blast, which was heard twenty miles away and blew out windows in houses in outlying settlements such as Attenborough, Chilwell and Long Eaton, several miles from its epicentre. It was a human tragedy of unprecedented proportions, and even today it remains on record as the biggest non-military explosion in British history.

The difficulty in precisely numbering the dead was not assisted by the fact that many of them remained only as assorted body parts; the only way in which the authorities could even attempt to calculate the dead was to consult the shift rosters of those who were believed to have been there, and subtract from that list the number of known survivors. Many of the workers were young women, and because the chemicals they worked with turned their exposed skin yellow, they were dubbed 'Canary Girls'.

There were many heroes of the tragedy, and a few who staggered away from it permanently maimed. But in respect of those who died there were no doubt many tales that could have been told of the lives they had led, the hopes and ambitions they had nurtured, and the events which led to those last, fatal, few moments.

Perhaps this is one of them.

CHAPTER ONE

The Encounter

It was the warmest afternoon of that June of 1968, but Dorothy Younger still shivered as she sat with her easel and paints amongst the old gravestones in the churchyard of St Mary's parish church in Attenborough. Hot flushes she could expect at fifty-four, or so her doctor had informed her, before adding that there was nothing he could do; perhaps if men had to go through the menopause they'd have found a more effective treatment by now, she reflected resentfully. But these shivers were new, and Dorothy was hoping that she hadn't caught a summer chill during her recent attempts to immortalise the local church in watercolours.

She shifted slightly on her camping stool in order to relieve the early onset arthritis in her hip, and as she did so she caught sight of something out of the corner of her right eye. She turned quickly, wincing in the process, and there, standing silently between two newer gravestones, was one of the weirdest sights she had ever encountered, even in her thirty-odd years as a teacher. It was undoubtedly female – the ample bosom which was barely held in check by the creased overalls was clear testimony to that – but the hair sticking out from under the front of what looked like a heavy-duty shower cap was green – yes, *green*. And whoever had advised her that a yellow face was stylish had obviously intended her no favours. The girl was no more than twenty-five at most, and she looked ridiculous.

"Please don't scream an' run away!" the figure pleaded with her.

"Why would I do that?" Dorothy enquired. More likely fall about laughing, she thought to herself. Her shrink kept telling her that she should appreciate the funny side of life more than she was naturally inclined to do.

"All the *others* did," the girl complained, "burra reckon yer a berrer bet than them, seein' as 'ow *you've* lost kids an' all."

Dorothy suddenly felt even colder, but from the inside this time. An abortion at nineteen, and a forced adoption after the alcoholism of her early thirties. But how did this weird girl know all about those? As if in answer, the girl smiled for the first time. She was lovely, in a plaster saint sort of way. Kind of old-fashioned looking, like a Van Dyck courtesan.

"I've seen yer 'ere *before*, ain't I?" the girl grinned, almost triumphantly. "Yer reckon that paintin's good fer yer mind, an' there's summat abaht this place that's bin drawin' yer dahn 'ere fer the past few weeks. Well, that were me."

"You seem to know an awful lot about me," Dorothy replied, guardedly. "How come?"

The girl smiled again.

"If I told yer that, yer definitely *would* run away. But if yer promise not to, I'll show yer summat yer may 'ave missed on yer previous visits."

Dorothy rose cautiously from her stool, and rotated gently in the manner her chiropractor had recommended.

"I could do with a break anyway; I can't sit for too long these days."

"Arthritis," the girl confirmed with all the confidence of an orthopaedic surgeon. "That's what yer gorrafter bein' pushed dahn them stairs. 'e were no good fer yer, that feller, but yer thought 'e loved yer, till it were too late."

"What exactly did you want to show me?" Dorothy asked frostily. This girl knew altogether too much about her, but it was as well to humour her. She might be deranged, and this was a lonely churchyard with only a few old cottages in the immediate neighbourhood.

"Cum wi' me," the girl instructed her, and waited while Dorothy narrowed the short distance between them, then turned on her heel and walked towards the far side of the churchyard, leaving a strong whiff of old-style perfume behind her. It reminded Dorothy of the Gardenia that her mother used to wear, years ago.

As she followed the girl she noticed the old-fashioned ankle length boots she was wearing, much shorter than the modern style, similar almost to the sort of thing her own mother might have worn. If the girl had just escaped from somewhere then they were very lax in the matter of personal dress, Dorothy concluded.

The girl stopped next to a tall solid wooden cross, to which was fixed a silver sword. On each side of the cross were two large graves, each bordered by low posts and chains and a series of what looked like stepping stones set into the ground. Between the two graves was a small metal plaque fixed to a simple stone plinth. The girl gestured with her hand for Dorothy to read it. It recorded that these were the graves of people killed during an explosion on July 1st 1918. Dorothy noted the date, and turned back to address the girl.

"Oh, I get it now. The fiftieth anniversary is just over a week away, and you're out to give it some publicity. You presumably belong to one of those historical groups who re-enact famous events, and I assume that your boiler suit and boots are some kind of costume depicting the event." Although that didn't explain the face make-up and the green hair, she added silently to herself.

"Yer'll prob'ly run away nah," the girl said, sadly, "burrav gorrer tell yer, 'cos it's important. I'm one o' them dahn there," she indicated with a nod of her head towards the graves, adding "at least, bits of me is. They only fahnd bits, 'cos we was all blown ter buggery."

Dorothy stared back at her, torn between open laughter

and the strong desire to escape from this lunatic.

"Don't tell me, this explosion turned your face yellow and your hair green, right?"

The girl grinned back at her.

"While yer tekkin' the piss, yer not runnin' away, anyroad. The yeller face cum wi' the job – all them chemicals we was usin'. As fer the green 'air, well yer got that if yer peroxided it, like I did. I were allus a vain bogger."

"This is all very interesting," Dorothy informed her in her best schoolmistress voice, "but I'm afraid . . ."

"Find 'im an' *tell* 'im!" the girl interrupted, pleadingly. "Find mi little Ernie an' tell 'im the *truth* abaht who 'is dad were! There's summat in it fer you an' all, if yer do!"

"I'm sorry – who's Ernie?"

The girl looked behind her, as if distracted by something. She began to fade before Dorothy's eyes, shouting, "I were Lil Jenkins. Find mi Ernie an' *tell* 'im! An' tell 'em all tharrit *weren't* Mabel what dun it!" before she was finally gone, leaving only an ominously empty space where she'd been standing.

Dorothy stood there in blank disbelief, suddenly afraid that she might have experienced another psychotic episode. It had been years now since she'd had her last 'difficulty', and Dr Meldrum had repeatedly assured her that if she kept to the medication, and foreswore the alcohol, she need no longer fear for her mental health. 'As daft as the rest of us' had been her precise turn of phrase, but then Karen Meldrum was a bit unusual in her approach to her patients.

But this was something else altogether. Dorothy dreaded having to report to Karen that she'd been all alone in a churchyard when she'd suddenly engaged in a conversation with a girl with a yellow face and green hair, who then disappeared before her very eyes between two grave markers. Her fears were heightened when she began to hear clicking noises behind her, and turned in time to see a furtive figure slip between two upright gravestones.

She remembered the Lithium tablets and the bottle of water she always brought with her when painting. She went back to where she'd left her bag, shakily extracted a tablet from the container and swilled it down with a large gulp of water. There was a movement behind her and she jumped round in fear, then yelled out in pain as the arthritis fought back.

"It's all right, dear," said the kindly-looking white-haired lady who stood watching her from the pathway. "It's only me, I'm Sarah Day, although almost everybody calls me Winnie. I'm the parish clerk at the church here, but you look like you've seen a ghost!"

"Maybe I have," Dorothy replied cautiously.

"Well, you wouldn't be the first, lately," said Winnie, "although I don't normally believe in that sort of thing. I've seen you here a few times, painting, haven't I? And as I came into the churchyard, I saw you over at the graves, where they buried all those poor souls from the explosion. There's always a funny atmosphere down there, and just recently folks have been reporting seeing 'things' flitting around the memorial. We've even been getting nosy reporters. But I dare say it's just people's overactive imaginations, what with the fiftieth commemoration service coming up soon."

"I noticed the date on the plaque over there. What exactly does it commemorate?" asked Dorothy.

"In 1918, there was a terrible explosion up at the shell-filling factory in Chilwell. It was wartime, and they were filling shells with high explosive. Then on the evening of July 1st, it went up with a big bang. There are still some people living around here who remember it. The old factory site's where the army depot is now, on the main road, and they'll be sending someone down from there for the commemoration service. Why don't you come along? It's a week tomorrow, at two o'clock. There'll be refreshments and everything."

"I might," Dorothy conceded, "but Monday's a school day, and I'm a teacher."

"Well, you'll be made very welcome, if you can find the time. And talking of time, I must get on and make sure that the church is ready for the evening service. Would you like me to show you around inside, while I'm here?"

"No thanks," said Dorothy. "I think I've had enough excitement for one day."

If Winnie was offended by the sarcasm in Dorothy's voice, it didn't show.

"As you wish, dear," she replied. "But I do hope to see you at the service. A week tomorrow at two o'clock." And she gave Dorothy a cheery wave, and continued down the path towards the church porch, jangling a set of heavy keys.

Dorothy made a note of the time and date of the ceremony on her partly completed draft sketch of the church, then gathered up all her remaining painting equipment, and, after a final reassuring look around the now deserted churchyard, got into her car and drove off in search of a strong coffee.

CHAPTER TWO
The best job in the area

Mabel Fletcher latched the front door quietly behind her and stepped out into the street. It was approaching five o'clock on a frosty Monday morning in February 1917, and she picked her way carefully down New Tythe Street, occasionally looking up to watch her breath escaping in cloudy bursts into the chill air. It was still fully dark, but the pale light from the gas lamps caused the frost to glint in patches on the pavement, and she didn't want to slip over again and miss a shift at work. Her father-in-law Sam had been really angry when she was five bob short in her wages, even though she was still well able to pay her digs money out of the remainder.

She turned right into Main Street, crossed the line by the level crossing next to the signal box, then turned sharp left again down the footpath they all called 'the twitchel'. It led half a mile or so alongside the Erewash Valley railway line to Trent Station, at the junction with the Derby to Nottingham line, with its small goods sidings where Sam worked, stencilling the numbers on the coal wagons for eight hours a day, six days a week. Her husband, Bert, used to work there too until the war started. Then he paid the price for his regular extra income as a Territorial, being shipped off to France in the first wave of Sherwood Foresters to defend Britain against the Hun. He was a lance corporal now, but that would mean little to his wife Mabel, and daughter Ethel, if he got himself shot or blown up in the trenches.

At least his letters home were more cheerful these days, and more frequent. The latest, stuffed in the handbag swinging from her right arm, had arrived only last Friday, and she had read it fifty times already. There'd been no leave for over a year, and some days she had to look at their wedding photograph on the mantelpiece in order to recall his happy, smiling face, and the mop of black hair which would never lie flat, even after a severe brushing. Ethel seemed to be taking more after Mabel, as her hair became longer and revealed the same light-auburn tinge.

From time to time Mabel looked behind her, anxious for a distant sight of Lil, hurrying to catch up with her as usual. At least she'd be welcome company down this dark footpath, and they often met up somewhere on this part of the trip to work, since Lil only lived a few streets away from where Mabel and her daughter were lodging with in-laws Sam and Vera Fletcher. "Just till this war's ovver, an' we gets back on us feet" as Bert had put it. That were Bert all over, she reflected. Nothing depressed his spirits for long, and he had hopes of becoming a signwriter with his own business, once the Kaiser had been put in his place.

There was still no sight of Lil as Mabel sat on the platform, waiting for the train to arrive and wondering where she was. They'd been close friends ever since they began work on the same day at the lace factory almost next door to where she was now lodging, two nervous fourteen-year-olds from nearby Phyllis Grove about to be introduced to the mysteries of overlocking and backstitching. That was how she had first met her husband Bert, as he and his father Sam returned home for their midday meal every day, past where the factory girls sat on the front steps eating their sandwiches.

Then, when she returned to work after having Ethel, Lil had excitedly told her all about the new jobs that were being advertised in a munitions factory over at Chilwell, where they paid an average of thirty bob a week for twelve-hour shifts, and even gave them two meal breaks with subsidised meals. With Bert away in the army, and only her wife's allowance from which to pay the few bob a week towards the household expenses at number seventy, she'd jumped at Lil's invitation to join her, and the two friends now helped to fill the shells which her husband and his mates were eagerly lobbing into German trenches, in retaliation for what Fritz had been lobbing at them for the past three years.

The platform signal rose with a resounding clang, and a couple of minutes later the Nottingham-bound train appeared round the sharp curve from Sawley Junction and screeched to a halt in a cloud of steam, and with the usual smell of hot oil and smoke. Mabel forgot all about Lil as she searched the carriages for the emptiest compartment. This was an all stations local train from Derby, and there were no corridors. Whichever compartment you got into, you were stuck there until at least the next station, but that was where Mabel would be getting off anyway so it didn't matter all that much. She found one that had only three people standing, besides the ten lucky ones crammed into the seats, and climbed in.

After only five minutes, during which she had at least been able to warm up a little in the press of the others sharing the compartment, she stepped down onto the long platform at Attenborough, walked back towards the level crossing, and after waving her free rail pass at the regular ticket collector, stepped out into Attenborough Lane for the final half-mile walk to the factory. Another train had just pulled in at the up platform, and the ticket collector had his hands full as even more workers began to stream over the foot crossing, merging with those who had just alighted from the Nottingham train. It was still only half-past five in the morning, but the lane was now full of workers heading for the No. 6 Shell Filling Factory, and another week engaged in what they called 'the war effort'.

Mabel had not even reached the main road when she heard the familiar voice behind her, calling her name. Lil clumped awkwardly up the lane as fast as her fashionable heels would allow, dodging and weaving in between the slower

workers, carrying a large shopping bag and puffing heavily as
she caught up with Mabel.

"Where the 'ell did *you* get to?" Mabel demanded. "I were
lookin' fer yer all the way dahn the twitchel, an' I couldn't see
yer on the platform, neither."

"I cum the other road," Lil explained breathlessly. "I were
on that Derby train. I spent the weekend wi' ar Doris an' 'er
man in Beeston, an' I gorron the train there."

"Yer bin shoppin?" Mabel enquired, looking down at the
shopping bag.

"Nar," Lil replied, "that's mi party frock. I went ter the
sojers dance in Beeston on Sat'day night, an' stayed ovver wi'
Doris. Almost missed mi train this mornin', mind yer."

"D'yer gerrof wi' owt decent?" Mabel asked, well aware
of Lil's record with handsome young men, particularly those
in uniform.

"Nar," Lil repeated, "but the singer in the band were right
good-lookin'. The Twilight Orchestra they was called, an' 'e
bought us a port an' lemon in the interval. I'm gunner keep
an eye aht fer wherever else they're playin' an' try mi luck next
time."

They paused to allow an early morning milk cart to trot
past them, then crossed the main road and carried on up the
lane towards the entrance gate to the factory, as a pale dawn
heralded its appearance over Beeston, to the east. As if on a
silent command, everyone joining the queue to the gate lit up
a final cigarette. To get through the gate, they were required
to hand them all over, along with matches and anything else
combustible. Where they were heading was not a good place
to strike a light, and if they were caught with 'contraband',
they could be hauled before the local court and fined, or even
imprisoned.

They shuffled slowly down the queue until they reached
the sallow-looking youth who was checking their work
identification discs, and handing back a numbered token for

each person's smokes, then placing them in a correspondingly numbered slot in the pigeon-holed shelf of the small hut in which he sat. As Lil handed over her cigarettes and matches, he grinned at her through his acne and handed her a numbered token.

"P'rhaps as well yer didn't try an' 'ide 'em in yer knickers, otherwise I'd've 'ad ter go lookin' forrem."

Lil ground the butt of her Woodbine into the ground, and fixed the boy with one of her defiant stares.

"Tommy Gardner, when yer mam does 'er next week's wash, yer'd berra tell 'er ter include yer mahth an' all. *An'* yer filthy mind, while she's at it, 'cos it's small enough ter go in wi' 'er unmentionables."

Those within hearing chuckled, and Mabel reminded herself yet again that it was not a good idea to mess with Lil when she was on her high horse.

Once inside, they clocked on and headed for the changing rooms, where they stripped naked and pulled on the shapeless overalls that went with the job. Since it was the first shift of the week, the women's supervisor had placed the first clean overalls of the week in front of the lockers of each girl on A shift, which was working days that week. She had also pinned the bath rota on the noticeboard; every member of staff was required to bathe at least once a week in the bathhouse that came with the remaining facilities on the two hundred acre site. For those without a bath at home, it would save an inconvenient trip to the public baths during their valuable off-duty hours, and personal hygiene was taken very seriously at the factory, given all the health hazards which came with working amongst lethal chemicals.

Another health precaution required all those working in what were called the 'danger buildings' – which included the mixing house where Mabel and Lil worked – to drink a cup of hot milk at the beginning and end of each shift. It was a cold morning, and for once they didn't grumble when the girl who had brought them from the canteen handed them out under the eagle eye of the women's supervisor.

Then it was on with the hated caps, which were intended to keep their hair out of the machinery; this was a doubly-wise precaution for Lil, with her long peroxide-blonde locks which normally cascaded over her shoulders. Finally, the pull-on boots, and then it was a matter of walking the short distance to the mixing house, where Mabel and Lil worked alongside each other. A week on days alternated with a week on nights. It had taken a little while to wangle themselves onto the same shift, and George Smedley, their shift overseer, who was responsible for all the mixing rooms during their twelve hours on duty, still had a downer on Lil for replacing Alice Mortlock, who now worked the B shift and was currently on nights. Rumour had it that George and Alice had a 'thing' going, and could often be seen entering and leaving the TNT storeroom together.

Lil was about to follow Mabel into Mixing Room No. 2, when George came bustling past her and turned to block her entrance.

"Before yer go in, there's bin complaints from the B shift that yer leavin' things in a right filthy mess. So I want yer ter mek sure everthing's left neat an' tidy, noronly in this mixin' room, burrin all of 'em. So just mek sure yer does. I'll be checkin' up on yer, so don't go thinkin' yer can pull the wool ovver *my* eyes – gorrit?"

"Yeah, sure," Lil retorted with an insubordinate grin, "an' while I'm at it, d'yer want me ter stick a brush up mi arse an' sweep the floor an' all?"

"Just gerrin there, yer cheeky bogger!" George replied. "It's ten past six, an' yer've done sod all yet."

There was less hilarity once they started the day's work. For one thing, they had to concentrate very hard to get the mix just right in the pans, before carefully transferring the final powdered mixture into the trays which were sent by overhead covered conveyor to the press houses, where further teams of girls would then carefully fill the converted oil cans which they used to pour the mixture into the open shells, before resealing them with fuses and detonator caps. Even if they got the mix right, there was the ever-present risk of an explosion, given the unstable qualities of the TNT and ammonium nitrate which were the primary ingredients of the mix, known technically as Amatol. Hence the minimum use of metal tools, to prevent the spark which would be all it needed to send the entire building into orbit.

In the main, they worked in nervous silence, and were paid five bob a week extra, as danger money, but they were always glad when it came to one of the two meal breaks, when they were all required to wash thoroughly and don white shifts before making their way along Chetwynd Road to the canteen. These one-hour meal breaks were always fun, the food was cheap and of good quality, and the workers constantly reassured themselves that they had 'the best job in the area'. Most days, weather permitting, those who preferred could lie out on the grass in front of the main offices, and listen to the factory band playing a selection of popular tunes. But for most, it was the good-humoured banter in the canteen that they looked forward to.

"I gorranother letter from Bert," Mabel proudly announced as she slurped another mouthful of tea to wash down her shepherd's pie during the second break.

"Where is 'e nah?" asked Nellie Bishop.

" 'e's norrallowed ter say, o' course, but 'e sez it's stopped rainin' anyroad, an' the parcels've started gerrin' through again."

" 'ave they 'ad any more o' that there gas?" enquired Tom Driscoll.

"Not that 'e said, burre's fed up o' them new gas masks, 'cos they mek a right mess of 'is 'air. Mind yer, it must be berrer than peein' on yer 'ankie, like they used ter 'ave ter do."

"Sojers never 'ad 'ankies in *my* day," complained old Jim

Booth.

"They didn't 'ave proper *guns* 'alf the time, neither," added Ted Buckley, a veteran of the Sudan campaign. "It's a different do this time, wi' all them shells flyin' arahnd."

"At least we're firin' 'em back nah," Lil commented. "Before they opened this place, they reckon that all the shells was comin' from the German side."

"They still are," pronounced a young former soldier invalided out of the trenches until he got used to life with only one arm, "an' yer never know when they're comin' till it's too late. Yer just 'ears this sorta whistlin' noise, then *kerpow!*"

"Shurrup, fer Christ's sake!" Mabel demanded. "Yer forgerrin' I've gorra man what's still aht there, gerrin' shot at! This 'ere letter's dated three weeks ago. Fer all I know, 'e could be dead while I'm sittin' 'ere readin' it."

"I'm glad I'm not the only one as gets that 'orrible feelin," declared another girl at the long table who had a fiancé in the same battalion as Bert. "Can't we talk abaht summat more cheerful?"

"Ey up, 'ere cums Mouldy Moreton," Lil warned them as she looked across at the entrance door. " 'e'll 'ave nowt cheerful ter say, anyroad."

The factory's day superintendent, Arthur Moreton, shouted as loudly as he could to get everyone's attention, then cleared his throat for the supreme effort of making himself heard above the combined clatter of over fifteen hundred people all eating at the same time.

"We've 'ad reports as some've ar shells is not goin' off proper. Duds, they calls 'em, but they're not sure why, 'cos no bogger's daft enough ter go inter the enemy trenches ter find aht." He paused for the anticipated laughter, which never came, then continued. "The best bet is the percussion caps; them's the flat things yer screws inter the shell after the fuses."

"Gerron wi' it, Mouldy!" shouted a male near the back.

"An' you mind yer manners ter yer superiors, Arnold

Pratt! Anyroad up, the word from White'all is ter check that
yer gives the caps at least six turns afore yer claim yer've done
the job. That's mainly fer the benefit o' the girls in the press
'ouses, o' course."

" 'e sez yer ter screw more often, Nancy," whispered a
young male trolley driver to the girl next to him, earning
himself a slap in the face which was heard all round the
canteen.

"But it's mebbe that the mix's wrong on some of 'em,"
Moreton persevered, "so don't the rest of yer go gerrin' slack,
neither. The word is that if we mek too many more duds,
there'll be some top brass dahn from White'all ter purrus in ar
places."

"The best place fer *'im's* in a bloody museum," Lil
whispered to Mabel, who tried not to choke on the last of her
tea.

The day after Dorothy's disturbing encounter was a Monday,
and during the morning tea break at Charlton Comprehensive
School she took her coffee and sat in the vacant seat next to
Phil Seaton, Head of History.

"Do you know much about local history?"

"I know that Forest went out in the semi-finals last
season, if that's of any interest."

"I was thinking of the Chilwell Shell Filling Factory."

"Apart from the fact that it blew up – in 1918 I think it
was – no."

"Yes, it was 1918. The fiftieth anniversary's a week today."

"I didn't notice your collecting tin," Phil observed
sarcastically.

"I'm just curious, that's all. I was down at Attenborough
yesterday, in the churchyard, and they're having some sort
of commemoration service on July 1st. I thought I might go

down and have a look, and it would be useful to have some more background on it. But still, if you can't help . . ."

"Hang on a minute," added Phil as Dorothy was about to get up and sit with Christine Pullman, her usual break-time companion, "*I* can't help, but I've got a good friend who probably can. Colin Buchanan, who heads up the newly formed Local History Unit at the university. He and I were at Leeds together, and he's a decent sort of bloke, apart from being a Scotsman who maintains that every British monarch after James II was an imposter."

"I don't need a lot; just the basic background information."

"Leave it with me. He owes me a pint anyway."

Three days later, during the lunch break, Phil Seaton walked purposefully over to where Dorothy sat at the communal table, marking third form science homework, and handed her three stapled sheets of paper.

"There you are! Next time you go on about men being useless and self-obsessed, think of me and experience shame and remorse."

She smiled her thanks, and put the papers in her bag for later. When 'later' came, she was seated on her couch at home, her legs tucked under her, sipping her second cup of coffee from the pot she had prepared earlier. The photocopied document which Phil had given her appeared to be the short introduction to a larger research document prepared by a master's degree student at the university, with a few faint comments in what had presumably been Colin Buchanan's pencil as he made notes in the margin. She was only interested in the main document, which read as follows:

What became officially known as National Shell Filling Factory Number 6, Chilwell, was the end product of painstaking and diligent work by Godfrey, 8th Viscount Chetwynd, who, during the so-called "Shell Crisis" of 1915, was charged by Minister of

Munitions, David Lloyd George, with the task of creating a factory to fill large calibre shells with a new experimental explosive known as 'Amatol', a mixture of TNT and ammonium nitrate which was easier and cheaper to procure than the purer TNT which was previously used.

These shells were urgently needed because the Allies were losing out to the Germans in fire power, and the Chilwell site suited all Chetwynd's needs. It was close to a railway line from which a siding connection could be constructed, and it was sheltered from its immediate neighbours by hills, and lay in a flat plain just north of the main Nottingham to Birmingham road. A further bonus was the availability, locally, of an abundance of labour, mostly female, made redundant after the wartime reduction in the traditional lace manufacturing industry in which most of them had been employed pre-war.

The first shells began to roll off the line in the first week of 1916, and by the end of its first year, Chilwell was turning out over fifty percent of all shells being shipped across the Channel. A variety of calibres of shell were filled at Chilwell, but it will be best remembered for the fifteen inch Howitzers which the Allies pounded into the Germans as they slowly began to retreat eastwards. It would be no exaggeration to claim that the workers of the Chilwell Shell Filling Factory turned the tide of the Great War, and fought the Kaiser to a standstill from deep inside a largely still rural part of England.

Ironically, shortly before victory was announced, tragedy struck at those brave men and women who had daily faced the risks attendant upon the handling of high explosive. On the evening of July 1st, 1918, a massive explosion, whose origins remain a mystery even today, ripped apart the main factory, and killed over 130 workers. The extent of the blast was such that windows were broken in Long Eaton, several miles to the west, and the explosion itself was heard over twenty miles away. Telegrams of sympathy were sent to the relatives of the dead by both the King and Winston Churchill, and a memorial was unveiled on the site by the Duke of Portland the following year.

By this stage, Dorothy was beginning to nod off, despite the coffee, but she came wide awake again as her eyes took in the final paragraph:

Another, smaller, memorial was erected that same year in the churchyard of St. Mary the Virgin, Attenborough, adjacent to two mass graves into which had been consigned the pitiful remains of those whose body parts had never been formally identified. The exact number of those buried there, and whether they were men or women, is not known for certain, but many of them were young women, the 'Canary Girls', so named because of the yellow skins which they developed after long-term exposure to the chemicals with which the shells were filled.

She sat, dumbstruck, but in a strange way relieved. If she *had* imagined the whole thing, at least her delusion had been an accurate one. But how could she have known about the yellow face, unless she had perhaps read it somewhere, sometime in the past, and had consciously forgotten it?

She dug out the bag she had been using the previous Sunday, and found the note she had made. Whatever the *real* nature of her strange encounter that day, she at least owed that poor girl another visit.

CHAPTER THREE
Honouring the dead

July 1st fell on a Monday that year, but Dorothy had no
difficulty in persuading her trainee to take the second form
double chemistry class, and by skipping lunch she was able to
slip into the churchyard just as the blimpy looking man in the
immaculate army uniform was drawing to the close of what
had probably been a very dreary address.

"And so we pay tribute," he was saying, "to the memory
of those who made the ultimate sacrifice in order to keep our
country free. At the going down of the sun, and in the morning,
we will remember them. Amen."

It was then the turn of a clergyman, who no doubt was the
local vicar, to invite 'all those assembled' to partake of the light
refreshments which had been laid out in a nearby marquee, in
which steam could already be seen rising from an urn manned
by two middle-aged ladies.

Apart from the obligatory local politicians, the only other
persons who seemed to have taken the trouble to attend were
an old man and woman with arms linked, as if to keep each
other upright, and a smarmy looking creep with a camera
slung around his neck, who was dancing around with footwork
that would have done credit to Cassius Clay, and who was
seemingly engaged in an attempt on the world record for the
number of shots one could fire off in thirty seconds.

But at least none of those present had green hair, Dorothy
consoled herself as she headed back towards the entrance gate.

"Hang on a minute!" came a voice from behind her. "I
say, excuse me!"

Dorothy stopped and turned, and her worst fears were confirmed. It was the creep with the camera, and he *did* mean her. She sighed, and waited until he sidled up to her, wreathed in smiles and perspiration, and pointing his camera straight at her face.

"David Smiley, freelance feature writer. Just wanted a full facial to go under the banner headline."

"You'll get a full facial from my fist if you take any shots of me," Dorothy retorted, and turned back towards the gate.

"You were here about a week ago, weren't you?" the youth insisted in a raised voice. "I saw you over by the mass graves, apparently talking to yourself. Except you weren't, *were* you? You were able to see them as well, weren't you? You're not the first, and I've got notebooks full of stories of folks who've seen ghosts in this churchyard in the past few months. If I could just get your name, and your story, I reckon I can get you in every decent paper in the East Midlands."

Dorothy walked back towards him, stopped a few feet short, looked around her, then lowered her voice.

"Piss off, sonny."

Undeterred, the youth kept up the sales pitch.

"I've had *heaps* of stuff in the local rags, and you'd look very nice at the head of the feature." He stared all too obviously at Dorothy, who was wearing a tight-fitting, power-blue trouser suit, eyeing her up and down. "*Very* nice, in fact," he repeated.

"If I craved immortality right now, I would be tempted to gain it by shoving that camera where the sun doesn't shine. Now leave me alone!"

"Come on, now, just one full frontal to go with all the others. *Lonely lady communes with the dead*, that sort of thing."

"I said, leave me alone! And take that damned camera out of my face!"

"Allow me," came an authoritative voice, and something brown and wooden smashed the camera out of the youth's hand and onto the grass.

"That was a bloody Nikon F3!" the youth protested. "I'll sue you for that!"

"Send the bill to the War Office," came the sardonic reply, as the blimpy looking man in khaki waved his walking cane one more time in the general direction of the youth's face. "But be warned, young man, if you annoy this lady once more, I'll use this cane to convert your nose into a rear collar stud. Now, *beat it!*"

The youth retrieved the remains of his camera, and appeared to be conducting a private memorial service of his own over it as he walked back to his car. The soldier turned to Dorothy and smiled as he handed her his card.

"Major Tim Mildmay, RAOC and 39 Command Workshops, REME. Sorry about that, but the press really get on my . . . well, let's just say that they annoy me intensely. I have to deal with them all the time, and they're the lowest form of life."

"Dorothy Younger, science teacher and much obliged to you for your gallantry."

Tim laughed. "Haven't heard *that* word since Cyprus – and it wasn't used by a Cypriot. Can I interest you in a cup of tea?" he asked, inclining his head towards the marquee.

"Thanks, but I'd better say no. I have to get back to work, and I prefer coffee anyway."

"They could probably rustle one of those up for you as well, if you smile and look holy enough." He paused briefly, then added, "Sorry, sarcasm is one of my worst faults. Are you here because of a relative?"

"No, just curious. Presumably you are here representing the military."

"Got it in one. The colonel's back up at the depot, unveiling something that looks like it was abandoned by Cleopatra in her hurry to leave Actium, and I got the short straw down here, talking to the dead – or what's left of them."

"But for all you know, they could actually hear you," Dorothy suggested nervously.

"Don't believe in all that tommyrot," Tim replied, then laughed deprecatingly and nodded towards the memorial. "But just listen to me! That word was in regular use when those poor sods bought it."

"At least 'bought it' is a bit more modern," Dorothy commented. "We used that phrase all the time in the WAAF in the 1940s."

He looked genuinely surprised. "I wouldn't have thought you were old enough to have been in that show. Unfortunately, I was; that's how I got to be handy with this walking cane. Look, are you sure you don't want a cup of tea or coffee? Or maybe something a little stronger? The Officers' Mess is only just up the road, and my driver's waiting for me out there in the lane."

"No, really. It's very kind, but I must be going."

"What you said just now about 'them' hearing me. I couldn't help overhearing what that little oik was drivelling on about. Did you *really* see a ghost here?"

"Perhaps not, but thanks for asking. Now, if you'd excuse me, I really am due back at work."

"If you change your mind about that coffee, my number's on that card. Don't lose it."

Dorothy waved a final farewell with the back of her hand, and on the return drive to school allowed herself a little giggle. To think that in her early fifties she was still being chatted up!

Mabel was surprised to find, when she clocked on for the day shift one morning in the first week of August, that the night shift were not already climbing out of their overalls in the female changing room. She was even more surprised to find them still in the entrance hall to the mixing rooms, but as soon as she and Lil pushed open the door it was immediately obvious that this was going to be no ordinary day. Apart from the night shift staff, there were two army men in uniform, one of them obviously an officer, and three men with white coats over their smart suits. George Smedley was only waiting for the day shift to arrive, and then he made the necessary introductions.

"The night shift've bin 'eld back so's yer can all 'ear what these important gentlemen've got ter say ter yer. It's abaht the mix, so please pay attention. All yours, captain."

The strikingly handsome officer twitched his moustache in a nervous gesture, and surveyed the assembled company.

"Ernest Weston, Captain, Royal Regiment of Artillery. The other gentleman in uniform is Bombadier Padgett, direct from the front line. From the War Office Scientific Section, Messrs Hughes, Grant and Hurcombe. We're here to talk to you about the new mix that we want to try out."

"What's wrong wi' the present one?" Lil enquired immediately, only to be met with a reproving look from George Smedley.

"To tell you the truth, we're not exactly sure," the captain replied, "but that was a *very* appropriate question." Smedley's face fell, as the captain continued.

"For some reason, some of your shells don't explode on impact. Putting it more simply, they don't go 'bang' when they land. That could be because of a faulty detonator, or it could be the powder mix, which as you all know is experimental. So we propose to try a variety of different combinations of TNT and ammonium nitrate, which is where we need your accurate and diligent assistance. It's vital to the war effort. There are far too many duds that fail to go off when called upon to do their bit."

"I've known *men* like that," Lil chipped in. Bombadier Padgett swallowed a guffaw, Mabel kicked Lil on the ankle, and George Smedley gave her a murderous look.

"Quite," murmured Captain Weston to himself, with a slight reddening of the face. "But what we need from you chaps is careful record keeping of which mixture you use for, say, a week, before you move onto the next mix."

" 'ow will yer know which shells've got which mix?" Lil asked.

"Another very good question," the captain replied. "As you know, the shells all have stencilling done as the final stage in the process. We're going to give them all stencilled code numbers, which will be noted down by the chaps on the guns before they fire them. That's why Bombadier Padgett's here, to advise on the numbering system."

George Smedley had a query of his own. "The staff's used ter doin' the one mix all the time. 'ow d'yer propose ter stop 'em gerrin' confused every time they 'as ter change the mix?"

"Not sure, exactly," Captain Weston admitted. "That's one of the reasons why we needed to talk to you chappies."

"Easy," Lil chimed in. "Yer just puts different sized box thingies on the ends o' the chute wotsits. The operator fills the box thingy the normal way, then when the box is full, opens a thingummyjig in the bottom, an' aht it cums, smooth as a baby's pooh."

Two of the scientific officers nodded to each other, and smiled. Weston was grinning from ear to ear.

"A splendid idea!" he beamed, "even if the imagery is a little basic." He turned his beam on George Smedley, and enthused. "I knew we only had to ask those who actually work the system! Mr Smedley, you must be a very proud man, to have such an impressive team working under your command."

Smedley forced out a smile. "She's one've ar most experienced," he muttered, almost under his breath.

The meeting broke up, and the shift commenced, only to be interrupted briefly by a uniformed messenger bringing a note from Captain Weston, inviting Lil to take morning tea up at 'the Big 'Ouse' – as the staff called it – during her first break at 9.30. The so-called Big House was not only the residence of Viscount Chetwynd himself, but was also used as a records repository and a reception centre for visiting 'brass'. Lil broke all the rules by keeping the appointment in her outdoor clothes, and it was well after eleven before she reappeared, slightly flushed, back in her overalls in the mixing room.

"All right fer some," Mabel complained.

"It pays ter advertise," Lil explained. "An' guess what? 'e's invited me aht ter dinner wi' 'im!"

"Ooh, lah-di-dah!" was Mabel's first reaction, then she added. "You watch yerself, mi gel. Yer know what them officers is like; keep yer 'and ovver yer fanny."

"So long as there's still room fer 'is 'and, an' all," Lil remarked, still slightly out of breath with all the excitement.

When the time came, Dorothy decided to make a clean breast of it. After all, not telling your clinical psychiatrist that you'd been suffering from hallucinations was a bit like taking a bath fully clothed. Even so, as she sat in the easy chair across the coffee table from Karen Meldrum and told her all about the churchyard encounter, she still felt awkward and stupid. Karen listened attentively, twiddling her glasses as usual, then got up and went back to her desk. She took out a document wallet from the top drawer and fished around inside it until she found what she was looking for.

"There, I didn't think I'd thrown it away. Violet Dunlop, psychic medium. No, don't look so alarmed, she's not one of those crystal ball types who reads tea leaves. She and I worked together as part of a research team at the local university, investigating human perception, and she was invaluable in sorting out *real* psychic experiences from autosuggestion and self-delusion. You need to know whether or not what you experienced was genuine, and she's just the person to tell you. I've used her before and I can assure you that there'll be no clanking chains, holding hands, or calling for signs from the spirit world. Now, do you want me to give her a ring and fix up an appointment?"

Just over an hour later, Dorothy parked her car outside the modest-looking bungalow in East Leake, and waved back at the kindly looking middle-aged lady who greeted her from her front doorway. Once her coat had been left in the hall cupboard, and she was seated at the dining table in the small rear lounge, Violet began.

"Karen tells me that you think you may have had a psychic encounter, and I want to put your mind at ease by reassuring you that if you have, then no harm can come to you if you just accept it for what it was. I've had to live with my so-called 'gift' for many years, and there are times when it's not easy. Imagine, for example, being at a dinner party for six, when you can see fifteen people round the table!"

"But this one seemed so real," Dorothy objected. "Not pale and shadowy, not something you could see through, no coloured lights." *Only coloured face and hair*, she reminded herself. Violet smiled back pleasantly.

"That suggests to me that you weren't self-deluding. People who self-delude tend to see what popular ghost fiction conditions them to see. Real spirit visitors look just like you and me."

"Even so," Dorothy countered, "I'm a scientist by education, and the discipline of physics and chemistry argues against all that."

"All *what*, dear?" Violet asked. "You scientists have laws, right? Laws of physics, principles of chemistry, mathematical formulae, and so on. Well, it's the same for spiritual communication, as well. For one thing, the recipient, if we can call them that, has to be of a certain receptive nature before they'll experience anything. You've perhaps been a sensitive all

CHAPTER THREE   27

your life, without knowing it."

"Sensitive, certainly," Dorothy conceded, "and in some ways oversensitive. But not in the way you mean."

"Well, let's see, dear. Ever experienced an unusual cold feeling swirling round you? Or a sudden breeze on a still day? A soft touch on your arm?"

"No," Dorothy replied, suppressing a shudder at the mere thought. She was aware of Violet concentrating on something just past her left ear.

"Your hair, perhaps? When you were a small girl, you had this habit of ruffling up your hair, but your mother liked to see it flat and straight, so she used to flatten it down again whenever she caught you doing it. You still occasionally sense someone's hand laid gently on your head, don't you?"

"Yes," Dorothy admitted, "but how did *you* know that?"

Violet smiled reassuringly. "Because your mother's standing right behind you, telling me all about it."

Dorothy whipped round, receiving a painful rebuke from her hip in the process. She yelped in pain, but she could see nothing behind her.

"Don't be afraid, dear, it's perfectly normal. Your mother's been in spirit for quite a few years now, hasn't she?"

"Yes, she died when I was only in my twenties, which as you can deduce without spiritual assistance was some years ago now."

"I thought so; her light's very dim. But she's very excited about something; she's almost agitated. I think she wants to bring someone through with her."

"I'd no idea I was so popular," Dorothy commented, for the sake of something to say.

"Hush for a moment, dear, while I concentrate," Violet requested, as she appeared to stare intently at the space just behind Dorothy. "This might be your grandmother. No, your mother's shaking her head. Anyway, it's a girl, apparently in her twenties, wearing a kind of boiler suit, and a bonnet of some sort. She's trying to say something about her face going yellow from chemicals."

Dorothy felt her blood chill, as she asked, "Lil?"

"No, dear, she says her name was Mabel. Mabel Fletcher. She's very disturbed, and she's gabbling so fast I can hardly follow her. Slow down, mi duck, please! That's better. She says she worked with Lil, and it was all her fault for being so selfish. Do you understand that, dear?"

"No," Dorothy replied, totally bemused. "But Lil was the girl I think I saw in the churchyard. And the way you're describing Mabel, Lil was dressed the same way, even the same yellow skin."

"She's fading now. It must be her first time through, and it takes a lot of practice, I'm told. But she's shouting the name Ernie. Does that mean anything to you?"

"That's my dad's name; at least, Ernest is. But he's still alive. Mind you, now I think about it, the *other* girl – Lil – she mentioned an Ernie."

"Well, bear it in mind for later, dear. And now they've both gone. Your mother shouted 'chin up, princess', just before she faded out completely."

A slow tear rolled down Dorothy's cheek.

"That was her favourite saying. I'm convinced now. How much do I owe you?"

Violet tutted. "I'm not one of those who charges money, dear. I just do it because I have to. They wouldn't leave me in peace if I didn't. Like I said, it's a mixed blessing being a sensitive. You've obviously got the potential, but if you take my advice, you'll stay well away from it. Now, shall I put the kettle back on?"

Dorothy waved her goodbye from the front gate, then got back into her car. She was home by just after four, and she looked out the card she had been given earlier that week. She dialled the number, and asked to be connected. When she heard the familiar voice announcing his rank before his name, she was in some ways relieved to be back in the real world.

"Major Mildmay? It's Dorothy Younger here. You remember, we met after the Attenborough ceremony on Monday? About that cup of coffee . . ."

CHAPTER FOUR

On the long long trail

"Ey up there, Mabel!" came a shout that threatened to wake half the street at five in the morning. Mabel waited patiently on the corner of Main Street, and watched Lil puffing towards her, face all aglow and wearing an ear-splitting smile.

"It's easy ter see *you* 'ad a good night," Mabel grumbled. "So go on; 'ardyergerron?"

"It were *magic*!" Lil enthused. "We 'ad proper chicken wi' all the trimmin's – *and champagne*! All served at the table bi some flunky in a posh uniform."

"And?" enquired Mabel cynically, as they crossed the line by the signal box and turned down the twitchel towards the station.

"An' what?" replied Lil, annoyingly.

'Cum on, gel – that sorta treat don't cum cheap. Wharrappened next?"

"Oh *that*? Well, we went fer a walk – just ter tek in the night air, as 'e purrit, an' we finished up in that wood just near the owd ghost 'ouse. Mi blue party frock'll never be the same again – all them grass stains!"

Mabel shivered. "Just the thought o' that spooky place meks mi 'air stand on end."

Lil giggled. "It weren't that what made 'im stand on end."

"An' did yer lerrim?"

"Lerrim *what*?"

"Lil, it's too early in the mornin' fer guessin' games. Did yer lerrim 'ave it?"

"Oh that. Yeah, course I did. I dunno if it were the

champagne or what, but once 'e got dahn ter it, I were that 'ot an' bothered that it just sorta 'appened, yer know?"

"Yeah, there's nowt wrong wi' *my* memory," Mabel remarked with a mixture of jealousy and sarcasm. "I 'ope 'e were wearin' summat."

Lil giggled again. "I seem ter remember that 'e kept 'is 'at on."

"Very funny. Yer know wharra mean. Were 'e wearin' a rubber?"

"Well, 'e said 'e were, burrit didn't feel like it. An' when I got 'ome, mi knickers told another story – good job I does mi own washin', else mi mam'd 'ave kittens!"

"Yer stupid cow! Wharrif yer fell fer a babby?"

"Nar, that's not likely. I only finished mi monthlies last week, an' they reckon yer can't fall until just before yer next one."

"You 'ope. 'onest, Lil, yer not fit ter be lerraht!"

"Well, that's where yer wrong, fer once. I'm seein' 'im again on Sat'day night, an' we're goin' dancin' in the tahn. I won't see 'im after that, though, 'cos we'll be on nights next week, an' 'e goes back ter London on Wednesday, then ovver ter France again. But 'e sez 'e'll write ter me regular."

"Oh aye, they all sez that. Fer all yer know, 'e's writin' ter ten different girls in ten different languages. Cum ter that, fer all *you* bothered ter find aht, 'e could be married. Yer brains is in yer fanny, an' that's a fact."

"What's up wi' you, Mabel? I can tell *you* gorrahterbed the wrong side this mornin'."

"Oh, it's nowt really; just 'ad another row wi' Sam, that's all. Ethel crayoned all ovver the livin' room wall, an' Sam reckons I should be payin' fer new wallpaper. I told 'im I'm payin' enough already, an' then 'e started on abaht 'ow Joe doesn't 'ave kids what wrecks the 'ouse, an' I sez that were only becos Joe's firin' blanks."

Lil chuckled. "I bet that went dahn well."

She knew all about Mabel's fragile relationship with her father-in-law. The older brother, Joe, was the favourite son, since he'd 'gorron in life', and was now a foreman in a local ironworks which was doing very well out of the war, producing castings for munitions.

Mabel's husband Bert had in some ways rubbed salt into the wound by insisting that when the war was over, he intended to start out on his own as a professional signwriter, something Sam had tried many years before, but had finished up bankrupt. Now Sam's days were spent obsessing about money, and reflecting bitterly on the chances he claimed to have been denied. Every payday there was an argument about money, and every payday it was her mother-in-law, Vera, who had to step in between them. Vera idolised Ethel and worried incessantly about Bert, and these two factors were enough to bond the two women together against Sam's churlish attitude towards his second born and his family.

As they carried on walking down the twitchel, they were each thinking about something different when suddenly lights could be seen coming round the curve on the Derby line, and they heard the distant hiss of steam.

"Is tharrar train?" Lil asked.

"Bloody 'ell, yeah! Cum on, gel – time ter run off some o' that chicken!"

Dorothy kept an eye on the entrance as she sat in The Copper Kettle Restaurant in Attenborough, studying the menu and wondering whether to throw all caution to the wind, ignore her doctor's warnings, and order a selection of the delicious home-made cakes temptingly displayed on the sweet trolley. It was Saturday morning, and as she waited for Tim to arrive, she pondered on why she was here in the first place, instead of doing her usual weekly shop. The answer came out the same every time; Violet had made it very clear that if you ignored demands from 'them', they only got more insistent, and she wanted no more encounters like the last one, in a churchyard, or anywhere else for that matter. Lil Jenkins wanted her to find someone called Ernie, and now another one called Mabel Fletcher seemed to have got in on the act. Dorothy knew that if she didn't at least make an effort, they'd *never* leave her alone.

He came through the door, looked around, then spotted her, waved, and began to limp over to her table. At least he wasn't wearing his army uniform – at least, not quite. But he still carried his gold-topped officer's cane. And the all too obvious regimental blazer and tie – which he had chosen to go with the grey flannels – left no-one in any doubt that this was a military type on a morning off. He smiled when he reached the table.

"Do you mind awfully if I take this seat with my back to the window? That way I can stretch my gammy leg out fully without tripping up any waitresses."

"Not a problem," Dorothy assured him. "War wound?"

"Depends how you define wound, I suppose. Left half my right leg on a beach in Normandy and never thought to go back for it." He lowered himself gently into the chair, propped his cane against the table, and picked up the menu.

"Never been here before – the cheese scones sound good. What are you having? My treat, by the way."

'Just a black coffee, if that's OK, and perhaps a currant bun. I was tempted by those cream cakes, but I have to watch my figure."

"Along with all the blokes, you mean? Sorry; poor taste." He waved his hand at a passing waitress and ordered a pot of tea and two cheese scones for himself, and a currant bun and a black coffee for Dorothy.

"Assuming you were referring to the Normandy landings," Dorothy said in order to keep the conversation flowing, "I was on duty for forty hours straight at RAF Harwell during that op, sending in the advance airborne chaps in their gliders."

"Some of them actually reached their target," Tim observed, "but the entire operation was a total shemozzle. Don't believe what the army propaganda films said; it was a total cockup from start to finish! I was in the gold mob, and the landing craft commanders refused to go right in because of the snipers in the buildings at the back of the beach. The men were ordered over the side into twelve feet of water, with ninety pounds of kit, and holding their rifles above their heads. I lost more of my company to drowning than I did to enemy fire."

Dorothy sensed the need to lighten things up a little.

"So they gave you a safe desk job after the war?"

"Yes, Major in RAOC, and now attached to REME at the same time. Strictly non-combat record keeping. Unless you regard constant aggro from senior NCOs as some form of combat in itself."

"Record keeping," Dorothy repeated. "That could be just what I'm after." Tim frowned.

"You mean it wasn't just my sparkling personality which grabbed your attention? Let me guess; you're working for Kremlin Intelligence, and they urgently need to know how many box spanners we keep in the workshops central store in case they decide to invade tomorrow."

Dorothy decided to reward him with a smile, in the hope that she hadn't already been too obvious.

"Not exactly, but I like your thinking."

At that moment, the waitress brought their order, and Dorothy waited until Tim had loaded his first scone with butter, and had the first piece in his mouth, before she continued.

"Actually, do you have anything on that explosion you were commemorating on Monday?"

"There are boxes full of it, since you ask. I'm only up here on a medium-term secondment, to supervise the transfer of all the records. Did you know the whole depot's going down to Bicester, shortly?"

"No, I didn't. But I'm researching two girls who may have been among the dead. Lil Jenkins and Mabel Fletcher. Have you got a full casualty list?'

"Not only me, but half the local historians in the county. That information's been in the public domain for years. The names of the dead are actually on a memorial at the depot. If you're interested, I could fix you up with a gate pass."

"I'm a scientist, not an historian," she reminded him. "I think that the two I'm interested in may be among those body parts in the graves at Attenborough Church. Lil Jenkins and Mabel Fletcher; did you want to take notes?" she hinted.

Tim pulled a notebook and pen from his blazer pocket and made a note of the names.

"Well, most of those killed were never actually identified. But you just want to know if they're on the missing list, right?"

"Something like that. Just anything you can tell me, really."

"OK, here's the deal. I'll give you all the lowdown I can find on those two, if you give me some more information about yourself. Married? Divorced? Single? Off men completely?"

"All but the first," Dorothy informed him. "Married twice, in error. Divorced twice, at considerable emotional expense. A daughter somewhere in the world who might one day prevail upon the adoption authorities to put her in contact with me. A science degree from Oxford, mainly to piss off a father who taught at Cambridge. Your line of work, actually, 'strategic studies', it was called. I was the black sheep of the family, but my elder sister took a law degree from Cambridge, then hung around doing nothing until she found a boring solicitor who was prepared to tie the knot in her personality. So there you have it. I teach science for a living, read Agatha Christie, listen to Brubeck for pleasure, and spend my Saturday mornings drinking passable coffee with attractive mature army officers. Now, what about you?"

"Divorced one less time than you. Once engaged to the most beautiful dancer you ever saw, who decided that she preferred men with two legs; then married to a hard-nosed bitch who spent most of her life digging holes in the Egyptian desert before she had a torrid affair with a museum curator and left me the bill. You don't have a monopoly on bitterness and cynicism, as you may have noticed. Did you mean what you said about 'attractive', by the way?"

"Attractive in the sense that you haven't tried to drag me off to bed - yet."

"I don't regard either a local churchyard or a main street coffee shop as suitable backdrops for seduction. But when I hand over the information you've requested, it'll cost you lunch."

"You obviously haven't sampled my cooking. I'm no Fanny Cradock, but I can rustle up a passable meal if pushed."

"I meant a pub, actually. They do a decent ploughman's at the Cadland in Chilwell, just up the road there."

"Next Saturday?" Dorothy suggested. "I teach all week."

"Saturday it is, then. I'll misspend next week getting all the gen I can on your two ladies, and miss you while I'm doing it."

"Now don't go spoiling it." She allowed herself to smile as she stood up and placed a piece of paper on the table in front of him. "Here's my home phone number. As of this moment, I have an urgent appointment at Fine Fare, so I'll say thanks again for the coffee, and bid you a fond farewell."

She was conscious of his appraising stare burning a hole in her bum as she headed for the door.

"Jesus bleedin' wept, fuckin' socks again!" complained Claude

Simpson. "Looks like these were knitted bi mi mam – they'd fit one o' them fuckin' cart 'osses what pulls the eighteen pahnders. I asked fer more mittens, an' I gets bleedin' socks! What d'you get, Fletch?"

Lance Corporal Herbert Fletcher grinned back at him through the drizzle.

"More o' mi mam's 'ome-made jam, plus another picture o' the missus an' kid. Oh yeah, an' some mittens an' all. Sorry, Simmy."

The usual early morning exchange of artillery had ceased long before the rain returned, and the supply lorries had, for once, made it as far as the second line. It had once been the German front line, and before that the Allied front line, and before that no-one could quite remember. It was late September in 1917, somewhere in the middle of nowhere recognisable, and nobody seemed to give a shit any more.

They were squatting down below the parapet, on the duckboards which the sappers had installed only two days previously, and which already had enough dead rats embedded in them to constitute a sort of carpet. They had placed their rifles to the side as they eagerly ripped open their parcels, and they were still examining the last of the wrapping in case they had missed anything when a pair of brown shoes hove into view around the corner from the privies.

"Why aren't you men at your posts?" the officer demanded.

"We was just openin' ar parcels from 'ome, sir," Private Simpson began to explain.

"I could have been a *German*!" He glared at Bert Fletcher. "You – the lancejack. Did you get that stripe opening parcels?" Bert went pale in the face, and took a few obvious deep breaths, before replying.

"No, sir. I got this 'ere stripe 'cos I were the only one left in mi company after we was sent ter capture this 'ere trench what 'eadquarters told us were empty. It were full o' Fritz, an' the lancejack whose stripe I got is still in that there barbed wire."

He indicated with a jerk of his head towards a rotting carcass draped over what had been a German defensive stretch of barbed wire. It was covered in flies, and was only a matter of a hundred yards from them. There were others dotted down the wire, along with assorted arms and legs. The officer was clearly unimpressed.

"Your name?"

"Lance Corporal Fletcher, sir."

"I'm Captain Bruce, and your newly re-formed company is now part of my Second Battalion, Eighth Division. We're moving forward in twelve hours, chasing the Hun right back where he came from. See to it. And I'd advise you, lance corporal, to mind your tone when addressing an officer."

"Yes, sir. Certainly, sir," Bert replied.

They waited until he was well out of earshot before bursting out laughing. Bert let out a loud fart, and stuck two fingers up in the air.

The telephone rang just before she retired for the night the following Thursday, and she grabbed it eagerly. She breathed a sigh of relief when she heard the voice.

"Dorothy? It's Tim here. I can call you Dorothy, can I?"

"Of course you can, if I can call you Tim."

"Permission granted. Are we still on for Saturday?"

"Of course. Let's say one o'clock, that way I can get my groceries in first."

"Something healthy and wholesome I hope."

She allowed herself a chuckle, then got down to business. "Did you get that information I wanted?"

"Not half. Got it 'in spades', you might say. You've really opened a can of something here, and it's not processed peas. When you join me for lunch, you'd better bring Agatha

Christie with you, because there are at least three mysteries in one for her to solve.'

"OK, Saturday at one then. The Cadland, wasn't it?"

'Yes, in the lounge at the back. See you there."

"Looking forward to it," she confirmed as she put down the phone. But as she slipped into bed, she was still asking herself whether she was looking forward more to getting the information, or to meeting Tim again.

Steady on, girl; not again! she told herself.

CHAPTER FIVE
At the starting gate

"Over here!" He was sitting in the bay window, waving her over to where he had saved a table. The pub was busy, and the smell of food was tempting. So was the thought of alcohol, but she had been warned off that by two doctors. Life really was a shit, she concluded, as she walked over to his table, on which he had placed what looked like quite a well-filled folder.

"No, please don't get up," she insisted, and took a chair facing both him and the window. The early afternoon sun brought out the silver in his no-nonsense, salt and pepper haircut. Still, it was better than the long black greasy stuff that she had once admired on Marco, she reminded herself.

"I haven't ordered yet," he told her. "I meant what I said about the ploughman's, and I can just as easily order two."

"Actually," she said, "I think I'll just settle for a packet of crisps – cheese and onion or salt and vinegar. Although my fascist doctor would even disapprove of that."

"I'm not your doctor, of course, but I'd say you needed to eat more, if you want to keep that cuddly figure."

"Cuddly! Is that some new sort of chat-up line these days?"

"Not guilty. Look, just give me a second, and I'll organise lunch. What will you have to drink?"

"I'll just have a glass of soda water and lime, if I may. Doctor's orders again."

"You should change your doctor," Tim advised her as he pushed himself to his feet and headed to the bar. He returned with a tempting-looking plate of baguette, butter, cheese and pickled onions, and a bag of crisps for Dorothy, and lost no time in tucking into the large lump of cheddar.

"It's rude to talk with one's mouth full," Tim remarked, "or so my mother always said. That was the only time we got any peace from her, so I've always believed it. Let's just finish our food first, because once we get started on this lot," he said, glancing down at the folder on the table, "we'll have no time to eat."

They ate in almost monastic silence, and Dorothy caught herself noting Tim's mannerisms. For a start, he appeared to be left-handed. He also chewed everything many times; no doubt another of his mother's strictures. *Stop it*, she told herself. You hardly know the man, and it's rude to stare.

Eventually they had both finished eating, and he opened the folder.

"Hard to know where to begin, and these are not just the records from the explosion. Once I started, I was so intrigued that I pulled out the entire personnel files on both of them."

"They had personnel files in 1918?"

"Of course. Mind you, they'd be as useless as tits on a bull. Oh, sorry about that; blame it on my coarse service life. As I was saying, they'd be pretty useless now, were it not for the fact in the early sixties the entire RAOC started switching over to a magnetic tape system of record keeping, and they decided to train up the data entry people by letting them archive old personnel records. Ergo, we have a printed sheet from 1918 for everyone who was working there then."

"Impressive."

"Yes – and no. Even so, there are huge gaps, and question marks thirty feet high. You couldn't have picked two worse examples with which to test the system. Are you sure this isn't personal? It's just that I noticed that one of the names of those killed had the same surname as you. I thought it might be your father or someone."

"No; my father's still alive, if you regard living in a nursing home with senile dementia as some sort of life. He spent his entire career in the Cambridge area, and survived the Great War as a distinguished army officer; or so he kept reminding us."

"Well anyway, here's where the mystery begins. The first thing I did was have a look at the memorial at the depot to check the two names you gave me, the girls you thought might be buried at Attenborough, and guess what? Neither name appears there. And then, according to the records, we have one of the girls at the centre of the explosion who walked out of it without a scratch, and the other girl missing from that day onwards who was over two miles away from the bang."

"What?"

"Let me begin by explaining the system to you. There were two twelve-hour shifts a day at the factory, starting at 6am and 6pm, and the explosion happened about an hour into the night shift. Mabel Fletcher and Lillian Jenkins – obviously the same person you referred to as Lil Jenkins – lived in the same house in Long Eaton, and had worked alternate shifts ever since Lillian came back from maternity leave. The records show that Mabel Fletcher was on duty that night, but the following day she was located in the family home, tucked up in bed with the flu. She gave a totally unconvincing story about having narrowly missed the bang, and having walked home in a daze without reporting her survival to anyone at the scene, which, I should add, looked like 'the morning after' in downtown Hiroshima, from what I've seen of the photographs!"

"And the other one – Lil Jenkins?"

"There lies an even bigger mystery. Lil worked the day shift and finished at 6pm, an hour before the explosion, but was reported missing by her mother a day or two after the bang. She'd been living with the Fletchers for some time, apparently, but they hadn't seen fit to report her missing, not even to her mother. Naturally, suspicion fell upon the

Fletchers, particularly Mabel because of her dodgy story, but Mabel then added another ingredient to the as yet unsolved mystery by dying during the flu epidemic that year. So you can see why I suggested that you bring Agatha Christie along!"

"You mentioned that Lil had been on maternity leave. When was that, and did the other one, Mabel, have maternity leave at around the same time?"

"Hang on, let me check." He rustled through several papers in the folder, then looked up and shook his head.

"No, just the one, Lillian Jenkins, from the beginning of March to the beginning of June 1918. The three-month period was a compulsory one imposed by the War Office for health reasons at the time; two months before the birth, and one month after."

"So her baby would have been born in about May of 1918?"

"So it would seem."

"And what about the baby's father? I assume Lil was married."

"There's no mention of a husband; in fact nothing about the father. That's another mystery."

"And the Mabel girl. She worked right on through this period – no maternity leave recorded for her?"

"Nope. She already had one child, it seems, a daughter. Her husband was away in the trenches, like so many men at that time. But why all the interest in the baby, anyway, when there's so much else in all this crying out for investigation?"

"It might just be the key to the mystery. If you've read any Agatha Christie, you'll know that the motive for the dastardly deed is nearly always some human weakness like sex, or love for a child."

"You think of those as weaknesses?" Tim looked genuinely horrified.

"No, not in the way you mean. But invariably, once Miss Marple, or whoever, uncovers the killer, the motive is usually a past love affair or the existence of some long-lost love child. I think I might start by checking out Lil's baby."

"You think it might have been the child of this husband of Mabel Fletcher?"

"Something like that. And if Mabel really *did* do away with Lil, it would be a perfect motive, wouldn't it?"

"I suppose so, but where are you going to start?"

"Births, Marriages and Deaths. I assume that Long Eaton has a Register Office, and at least we should be able to find out who was named as the father. And while I'm at it, I might be able to find out a bit more about Lil and Mabel. You never know, it could throw even more light on the mystery."

"Sounds like a lot of work to me."

"It just so happens that the school breaks up for the summer holiday at the end of the week, so I've got all the time in the world. And a perfect excuse for ducking out of yet another boring month on the Norfolk Broads, in what my older sister chooses to call her yacht, accompanied by her insufferable prick of a husband."

Tim almost choked on the last of his beer.

"And to think I actually apologised to you earlier for saying tits! You'd not be out of place in the NCO's Mess up the road!"

Dorothy's face turned a deep red as she began to offer a profuse apology.

"Forget it," said Tim, still laughing. "It makes you even more attractive, somehow."

"D'yer want the rest o' mi egg sandwich?" Lil enquired as they sat in the canteen on the first break of the day. "Mi eyes must be bigger than mi belly."

It was the third week of October, and they were on the second day of a week on days.

"Aye, all right," Mabel agreed, taking the plate from Lil and swallowing the last of the sausage meat on her own plate. "Not like you ter be off yer food; yer could normally eat an 'oss between two mattresses."

"I bin like this fer a day or two. Musta bin that there pot roast mi mam made fer Sunday lunch. There were some rabbit in it, an' that allus giz me a gippy tummy."

"I 'eard from Bert again yesterday. 'e's got this bastard new officer what's givin' 'im an 'ard time aht there; as if the Germans wasn't enough. Talkin' of officers, 'ave yer 'eard from yourn?"

"Nar. I reckon yer was right abaht 'im; 'e's prob'ly forgot me already. Anyroad, time ter get back ter work."

Lil stood up, then went pale and gripped the edge of the table.

"Yer gunner spew, or summat?" Mabel asked, a look of concern on her face.

"No, I'm all right. Just went a bit light 'eaded there fer a mo. I'm OK nah, though; cum on."

Back in the mixing room, George Smedley was in a foul mood as usual. There were still complaints from the top brass about the level of duds coming out of the factory, and they'd ordered yet another variation in the mix. They hadn't yet supplied the necessary measuring devices for the correct amounts of TNT and ammonium nitrate to be dropped down the chutes into the mixing box, so they were having to estimate the proportions as best they could. It made life difficult for all of them, and difficulties were not George's speciality.

The normal way of working was for the measured amount of TNT to be pulled down via the chute from the ceiling, followed by the measured amount of ammonium nitrate. It was then mixed, and transferred carefully using large wooden ladles into the trays which were then placed on the conveyors that took them to the press houses. The speed with which they were able to supply the ever-hungry system depended entirely on how fast the girls could fill the trays.

It was an hour after their break when Mabel began to realise that Lil was slowing down, and that she appeared to be having difficulty in focusing while loading the trays. George Smedley started to notice after a while, too, and began chiding Lil for her apparent lethargy.

"Cum on, gel!" he cajoled her, "if we keep this rate up, we'll be well dahn on the day's tally!"

Lil smiled weakly, then slithered to the floor in a heap, unconscious.

Mabel raced over towards her, but George ordered her to stay by the mixing pan. He sent another girl – Clarrie – to the medical room with an urgent message, and five minutes later the nurse came with a stretcher carried by two burly men. They carried Lil carefully out of the room, through the main entrance lobby and down the road to the medical room in the Big House. George tried to keep Mabel back, but she invited him to "go an' fuck yerself", reminding him that Lil was her best friend, and followed the stretcher to the medical room in time to see Lil coming round on the examination couch.

The nurse was taking details, and after Mabel had confirmed Lil's name and date of birth, she asked her, "Can you think of any reason why she passed out like that? Has she eaten something that may have disagreed with her, perhaps?"

"I'm fine, 'onest!" Lil protested feebly from the couch.

"No yer not, gel," Mabel responded sadly, "I reckon yer pregnant." She turned back to the nurse.

"She were complainin' o' feelin' queasy durin' the fust break, an' she's bin gerrin' light 'eaded an' all."

The nurse turned to Lil.

"Have you missed your monthlies?"

Lil burst into tears. "I ain't seen owt fer two months. Mi mam'll kill me!"

"You leave yer mam ter me," Mabel insisted. "Right nah, we gorrer mek sure that yer properly looked after." She turned back to the nurse. "Will she 'ave ter go 'ome?"

"Oh yes," the nurse replied. "We'll let her recover in here and the doctor will do the necessary tests, but then she'll have to be taken home. And the regulations say she can't work here any more once she reaches seven months gone."

There was a wail from the couch.

"Shurrup, gel," Mabel told her. "Yer comin' 'ome wi' me."

"Wharrabaht George?" Lil enquired.

"No, 'e can bloody well stay 'ere," Mabel joked, "we ain't bringin' 'im an' all!" She was relieved to hear Lil chuckling back through her tears.

Dorothy had phoned the Register Office at Long Eaton to see whether they would be able to help her with her search, but was informed that all their old records were kept at the Ilkeston Office, and that is where she would need to go. The following Monday morning she found a parking spot on Bath Street and walked down Station Road to the Register Office. She went up to the public counter, and found herself confronted by an overweight man in a striped shirt two sizes too small for him, wearing a facial expression that suggested he might be recovering from some painful operation in the nether regions.

"Good morning. I'm trying to find out about some people who used to live in Long Eaton about fifty years ago. Is this where I can get details of births, marriages and deaths?"

"Depends," he muttered, unenthusiastically, "do you know exactly when the events occurred?"

"The events?"

"The births, the marriages and the deaths, of course," he said, tersely. "Do you know exactly when and where they took place?"

"Well, not *exactly*," replied Dorothy, rapidly becoming as

tetchy as he already was. "If I knew that, I wouldn't need to be here, would I?"

"Wait there a moment," he said, turned round and vanished into an office at the back.

After a few minutes, and no further sign of the man, a young girl appeared and asked if she could assist, her manner as helpful and friendly as her colleague's had been surly.

"Thank you so much," said Dorothy, and proceeded to repeat her request for advice, adding, "and you might like to lend one of your beautiful smiles to your colleague with the striped shirt."

"Oh, take no notice of him. He's only here temporarily and he *never* smiles," the girl confided. "He supports Derby County."

Once Dorothy had told her what she was after, the girl explained the procedure.

"Provided the birth, marriage or death was registered in Long Eaton we should be able to find it, as we have all their old register books. We need the name, of course, and approximate date, and an address also helps; in fact the more information the better. There's a charge of £5 for a certified copy."

"I see," replied Dorothy. "The problem is, the information I have is a bit sketchy. What I'm trying to find is a bit complicated and I don't have the exact dates or addresses. Now, if I were able to actually look through the registers *myself*, I might just find what I'm after, but I don't suppose that's possible."

"No, I'm afraid not. We're the only ones allowed to do that, but don't worry, we can still help you. You can make an appointment and come and spend all day searching the indexes. If you find what you think you're looking for, I can then go and check the details in the original registers. It'll cost you £12 for the day, then £5 for each copy."

"Right. That sounds OK. When can you fit me in?"

There was a free day on the Wednesday, and by ten

o'clock Dorothy was once more back at Ilkeston and found herself seated at a large table in a rear office. She had spent the previous evening working out what she wanted to discover – the date of Mabel's wedding and any mention of a Lillian Jenkins getting married; confirmation of when Mabel had died and the cause of her death, and the same for Lillian, if possible; the birth of Mabel's daughter; but most importantly, the name of Ernie's father.

She'd jotted these down in a notebook, along with her estimated dates for these events, and the helpful girl soon brought out the appropriate index books, one for each quarter of the year. These contained lists of names and it was simply a matter of searching through these until something of interest was found.

She guessed that Mabel had got married about 1912 – 1914, and started looking for suitable references. Finding nothing in 1912, she moved on to 1913, and soon found a Herbert Fletcher who was married at Long Eaton in about August 1913, spouse's surname Robinson. No other possible marriages could be found so she made a note of this one.

She decided to try and find the death dates next. Tim had already found that Mabel was still alive two days after the explosion, but had died in the flu epidemic of 1918. She turned to the death indexes for July to December 1918. You never know, she thought, she might even find Lil. She didn't have to look far before she found what she was looking for – Mabel Doris Fletcher, aged 24, died about July.

Poor Mabel, she thought. Less than half her age, married with a daughter, probably never been far and done nothing with her life, other than work from morning till night, husband up to his knees in freezing mud in the trenches and then – life over.

She spent another half-hour, searching until the end of 1919, but still no trace of Lil. The only Jenkins deaths were a George, aged 73, and a five-year-old named Myrtle.

So, giving up on finding Lil in the death indexes, she moved onto births. Assuming that Mabel and Bert's daughter had not actually been born *before* they had married, she started searching at about the time of their wedding – it was no secret that many brides walked up the aisle with a bun in the oven.

She searched the indexes from 1913, but by the time she got to 1915, the only Fletcher births she had found were three boys. She decided to carry on to the end of 1916 and then go and have a coffee, and was glad she did. For by the time she sat down in a nearby café with a black coffee and a cream cake – she deserved it whatever her doctor might say – she had found the daughter. Ethel Fletcher, born about July 1916, mother's maiden name, Robinson.

One more piece of the puzzle found, one more left. She was enjoying this, and was soon back at the Register Office and raring to go. From what Tim had discovered, Ernie must have been born about May 1918, so this should be easy.

Ernie, or Ernest, was obviously a popular name in those days, and she noticed quite a few, but none with the surname Jenkins. She checked again, to see if she had missed it; but she hadn't. In fact, there hadn't been many Jenkins births in Long Eaton, and certainly not an Ernie.

Disappointed, she sat for a while, pondering, when suddenly an idea came into her mind. Tim had told her that the records he had uncovered seemed to be confused about the two girls' identities, one of them apparently at the centre of the explosion but who walked out of it without a scratch, and the other missing from that day onwards. Could there have also been a mix-up over Ernie's birth registration, she wondered. Oh well, nothing ventured, nothing gained, and she'd paid her £12 so she started looking for the birth of an Ernie Fletcher.

"Eureka!" came the cry some minutes later, to the consternation of the overweight man in the striped shirt, who had reappeared that day and was keeping a beady eye on her. There it was – Ernest Fletcher, born about May 1918, mother's maiden name, Robinson.

But that couldn't be right, surely? The girl who had had the maternity leave – and presumably the baby – had been *Lillian Jenkins*. To make any sense of this, either the personnel records had got it wrong, and *Mabel* had been the one on maternity leave, or Mabel had gone to the Register Office and taken the credit for Lillian's labour, posing as her. Or Lillian had posed as Mabel at the Register Office, thereby getting away with registering Mabel's husband as the father of her child, and nobody any the wiser. Especially poor old Ernie himself, of course. Whose child *was* he – and where had he been brought up?

Confident she had found the right records, she ordered the four certificates and handed over the £20 – best purchase she'd made in months, for these would show much more information. The girl kindly offered to copy them immediately, and within thirty minutes she had extracted all the details from the original registers and made copies of each one. She handed these, sealed in a large envelope, to Dorothy, who thanked her profusely and headed straight back to the café for another coffee and slice of cake, and two fingers raised to the doctor!

Once she had taken a sip of her coffee, she opened the envelope and examined each certificate carefully.

On Saturday 23rd August 1913 at Long Eaton Register Office, Herbert Johnson Fletcher, bachelor, aged 21, railway shunter, of 70 New Tythe Street, father Samuel, also a railway worker, had married Mabel Doris Robinson, spinster, aged 19, lace hand of Phyllis Grove, father deceased. And then she noticed the names of the witnesses. One of them was a Lillian Jenkins – the name of Mabel's best friend, the third character in this mysterious triangle.

The death certificate showed that Mabel Doris Fletcher, aged 24, munitions worker, of 70 New Tythe Street, had died on 6th July 1918. Cause of death was influenza and the informant, present at the death, was Vera Fetcher, who Dorothy assumed was her mother-in-law.

Bert and Mabel's daughter, Ethel, had been born on 15th July 1916, also at 70 New Tythe Street.

And, finally, the one piece of information she really wanted to find. According to the birth certificate, Ernie, or Ernest to give him his full name, had been registered with the surname Fletcher, not Jenkins. He had been born on 4th May 1918, again at 70 New Tythe Street, Long Eaton. The father was named as Herbert Johnson Fletcher, Lance Corporal, BEF, France, the mother Mabel Doris Fletcher, munitions worker. Birth registered by the mother on 6th May 1918.

As she drove back home, she wondered where the truth lay. The certificates had given her a good deal of information. But who really was Ernie's mother? At least she could report some progress to Tim when they met for lunch again on Saturday. Same time. Same place. Same stupid schoolgirl tummy flutters just thinking about it.

"Well, I 'ope she'll be payin' fer 'er board an' lodgin' while she's 'ere."

"No, Sam, *I'll* be payin' forrem," Mabel retorted. "Lil's mam's a widder, an' she relies on Lil's money every week."

"She should've thought abaht that, afore she gorrerself in the puddin' club."

"Sam!" Vera protested. "Hush, she might 'ear yer. She's only upstairs."

"Aye, an' that's summat else. Where's she gunner sleep?"

"Wi' me, where d'yer think?" Mabel replied. "An' when the babby's born, *it* can sleep in there, an' all. Don't worry, yer'll get yer money every week."

"What's ar Bert gunner say when 'e cums 'ome on leave?"

"Considerin' 'e ain't 'ad no leave in ovver a year, I reckon we can worry abaht that when it 'appens," Mabel snapped back testily.

Mabel had, as usual, taken care of everything for Lil. She'd insisted, with support from a frosty-faced nurse who'd been more than a match for a very grouchy George Smedley, on coming back with Lil in the horse-drawn ambulance which the nearby barracks had been able to produce, had tucked Lil up in her own bed at number seventy, and had then gone round to Phyllis Grove to tell Mrs Jenkins that she was to become a grandmother sometime in April or May of the following year, that Lil would be staying for the time being with the Fletchers, and that she or Lil would call round every Sunday morning with Lil's weekly wage. Mabel didn't tell her that by March next year Lil would have no wage, but she'd worry about that nearer the time.

Ada Jenkins had first ranted and raved, then cried, then finally got around to asking how Lil was. She also got Mabel to promise to take the omnibus out to Breaston on Sunday, to tell her brother Willy, Lil's uncle, what had happened. Mabel kept her promise, but omitted to fulfil Willy's request to "tell the stupid cow that she'll 'ave 'er work cut aht when she's got a babby – an' there'll be no more o' that gallivantin' arahnd then!"

Finally, at the end of what had been a very tiring week, and with a week of nights starting the next day, Mabel sat down and wrote to Bert. As usual, there were kisses at the bottom. And as usual, there were tear stains on the envelope.

Dorothy was a little apprehensive of telling Tim, when they met next Saturday, that her search for evidence of Lillian's marriage or death had so far proved as fruitless as the monster investigations taking place at Loch Ness, which were currently receiving much coverage in the newspapers and on television.

But by then she had a new request for Tim, anyway. For on Thursday morning, her home phone had rung, and she had picked it up in the hope that it was Tim, confirming their lunch date. Instead, it had been Karen Meldrum, anxious to get hold of her with a message to ring Violet Dunlop.

"She sounded quite agitated – said she must speak to you as soon as possible."

"OK, thanks, Karen. I'll give her a ring straight away."

Violet picked up the phone on the second ring, and sounded very relieved to hear who was calling.

"Thank goodness it's you, dear. Perhaps I'll be able to get some sleep, now. They won't let you alone, you know, once they know that you can hear them."

"Mabel again?"

"No dear, a soldier this time. Says his name's Bert, and you'll know who he is. He mentioned Robin Hood, and I hope that means more to you than it does to me. But the message is, 'Check my leave dates'. Do you understand what he's talking about, dear?"

"Not at the moment, but I know someone who might. Leave it with me, Violet, and tell Bert that I'll deal with it on Saturday."

"Thank you so much, dear. God bless you."

The phone clicked down at the other end, and Dorothy smiled ruefully.

"God bless me? God help me, more like. What have I got myself into this time?" she said out loud to herself.

CHAPTER SIX

Keep the home fires burning

Vera set the plate of kippers down in front of Sam, and began carving slices from the cottage loaf in the centre of the table. Mabel had opted for a boiled egg, and Lil was having a lie down upstairs, and might have an egg later. The pregnancy was well advanced, but she seemed to be eating less and less as the day of the birth approached.

"Sometime this week or possibly next," the doctor had told them. Lil hadn't been working for over three months now, and there was the usual tension over money, even though Mabel was handing over all but a few shillings of her own wage, in order to keep Sam quiet.

"Thanks, Vera," said Sam. "Yer a good lass, allus 'as bin, though God knows yer 'as yer work cut aht, what wi' us, an' 'er up there," he added, with a jerk of the head towards the ceiling.

"Don't start," Mabel warned him. "We've 'ad all this aht before, an' Lil does what she can ter 'elp Vera arahnd the 'ouse."

"Aye, but she's not bringin' any money in, is she? An' don't remind me that *yer* payin' 'er board – it's the principle o' the thing. An' wharrappens when the babby's born, eh? I s'pose yer expectin' Vera ter look after that, an' all."

"As a matter of fact," Mabel replied with a self-satisfied smirk which somehow suited the egg dripping down her chin, "we've got that sorted aht. When Lil starts back after the birth, she's goin' on the opposite shift ter me. George were *very* 'appy wi' that, 'cos 'im an' Lil never saw eye ter eye, anyroad, an' 'e's arranged ter get 'is fancy woman back in 'er place, so it's all worked aht fine. An' while Lil's at work, I'll be at 'ome, an' viccy verccy. Between us, we can look after both the kids; an' just think, yer'll 'ave all that *money* comin' in!"

"Talkin' o' money," Sam added, with a swift glance across the table at Vera, who'd settled for some bread and dripping, "Vera an' me's bin talkin'. Am I right in sayin' that the army pays yer summat towards Ethel, as well as yer wife's allowance?"

"They tek it aht o' *Bert's* money, if that's what yer mean. God only knows, 'e's got nowt ter spend it on aht there anyroad, nah that the smokes is free. Why?"

"Well, what's ter stop yer claimin' fer *Lil's* babby an' all?"

"Yer mean apart from the fact that it ain't Bert's?"

"Yes, but *they* doesn't know that, does they?"

"I think Bert might notice," Mabel added sarcastically, "when 'e suddenly gets docked another couple o' bob a week fer a second child, when 'e's 'ad no leave fer a year. What's 'e gunner think o' me?"

"Yer could allus ask 'im," Sam countered. "Anyroad, yer said yerself that 'e's got nowt ter spend it on aht there, an' if the army's prepared ter give yer another two bob a week . . ."

"I just told yer!" Mabel retorted. "It's not the army what gives it ter me free o' charge; it cums ahter Bert's own pay!"

"Aye well, ask 'im anyroad. Abaht time the useless article did summat worthwhile."

Mabel slammed her teacup down on the table, spilling most of it on the lace tablecloth, and shot to her feet, her face already crumpling in tearful rage.

"That 'useless article' as yer calls 'im is fightin' fer King an' Country! That's you an' me, if yer 'adn't noticed! 'ow worthwhile would it be if 'e gorrimself killed? At least 'e's not sittin' on 'is fat arse in a so-called certified occupation like Joe. Yer mek me sick!"

She raced upstairs in floods of tears, as Vera looked reprovingly across the table at her husband.

"I think that were a bit 'ard, love," she said.

Upstairs, Mabel flung herself down on the bed and wept her heart out. Lil stretched out a comforting hand, and tousled her hair.

"I 'eard most o' that, I'm afraid. 'e can be a nasty mean bastard, that Sam, when it's owt ter do wi' money."

"Did yer 'ear what 'e said abaht the babby?" Mabel asked in gulps between sobs, as she sat up and searched in her blouse for a handkerchief to wipe her nose. Lil sat up as well, and placed a reassuring arm round Mabel's shoulder.

"Listen, mi duck, yer've all bin right good ter me, even that bogger Sam. I dread ter think what it'd be like, livin' wi' mi mam while I'm in this state. If I can repay yer all bi lettin' yer register the kid as Bert's, well where's the 'arm in that?"

Mabel had stopped crying, and was now thinking.

"At least it'd shut Sam's mahth up. I can't bear it when 'e goes on abaht my Bert like that! But, even assumin' Bert's agreeable – an' that's askin' a lot of 'im – well, we all 'as ter box clever. When the midwife cums, yer gunner 'ave ter pretend yer me, 'cos she tells the registry people, an' they waits fer yer ter go dahn there an' fill aht the papers. So we gorrer mek sure that the kid's got the right name even before the midwife goes back dahn them stairs wi' 'er notebook."

"Yer can leave the midwife ter me," Lil reassured her. "Yer've got the 'ardest job, persuadin' Bert tharris gorranother kid, at least on paper."

Mabel went back downstairs, and sat at the now empty dining table with paper and pencil.

My Dearest Darling Bert, she began. *This is the biggest favour I've ever had to ask of you, but mam and dad have asked me to ask you* …

In the Cadland, Dorothy had wrestled her conscience to the

ground and ordered a ploughman's lunch, promising herself
that she would live on grapefruit all next week. There was a
subtle change in body language, too, as they sat side by side
at the table, and Dorothy was reminding herself of how much
she liked the scent of Sandalwood aftershave.

"Of course I can get it, but I need a good reason. And I
need to know which regiment he served in, as well."

She had just asked Tim if he could gain access to Bert
Fletcher's service record, having faithfully reported her
findings at the Register Office. Tim looked far from happy with
this latest request, and Dorothy was searching her memory of
her last conversation with Violet Dunlop for something to add.

"He said something about Robin Hood. Does that help?"

"It certainly does! The 'Robin Hoods' were the Sherwood
Foresters. Infantry regiment, and from this part of the
country, as it happens. They would have been my first port of
call anyway, but that narrows it down a lot. But who is this 'he'
you just mentioned?"

Dorothy realised that she had just let a very large cat out
of a very embarrassing bag, but somehow she didn't want any
lies between her and Tim, so decided to come clean.

"You remember all that nonsense down at the churchyard
in Attenborough? Well, it wasn't exactly nonsense. You've
probably been wondering why I'm so interested in Lillian
Jenkins and the world she lived in, assuming that she's now
dead. Well, she *is* dead, and if you laugh at what I'm going to
tell you next, I'll slap you in the face and storm out of here, and
everyone'll think that you touched me up or something."

"Wouldn't dream of it. Laughing, I mean. Can't
guarantee the other thing, mind you."

"Later, perhaps," Dorothy was appalled to hear herself
say. "But how do I know that Lillian's dead? Well, here goes. I
talked to her ghost, spirit, apparition, or whatever you like to
call it, down there in the churchyard, a couple of weeks before
the anniversary. So now you can laugh."

"Not if it means getting my face slapped," Tim replied. "But why were you so reluctant to tell me that in the first place?"

"I believe the phrase you used when we met that day of the anniversary was 'all that tommyrot'. From which I deduce that you're a hard-nosed, practical type of person with no time for hysterical old ladies with crystal balls and Ouija boards. Why are you looking at me like that?"

Tim had suddenly gone pale, and from their close proximity Dorothy felt that he was trembling.

"I choose not to believe in the supernatural because I don't want to believe in it. But that doesn't mean that I haven't experienced it."

"Go on," she encouraged him.

"It was truly awful; the most distressing experience I've ever had, and bear in mind that I've been in the army all my life. It was during the Normandy landings. You remember when I told you about how botched the actual landings were, and how many men died?"

She nodded, and his voice fell as he retold the experience.

"Well, I was sitting up at the front of our landing craft. I was only a second lieutenant in those days, but all the men in the boat were under my command, although the person in overall charge of the boat was the naval type who was driving it. Anyway, just before we were ordered out into the water, I looked down the boat, and all I could see were, were . . ."

His voice broke, and his face began to crease with the effort of holding back tears. Dorothy took his hand and squeezed it gently, and he smiled back apologetically.

"Sorry for blubbing, but what I could see – *all* I could see – were skeletons in uniform! All my men; dead before we even jumped! When we got the order to go, I could see that the water was too deep, and I knew that half my men couldn't even swim, but, God help me, I repeated the order to jump. Some nights I wake up in a cold sweat, and I can still see all those skeleton faces; all the men who trusted me when I ordered them to jump to their deaths."

The tears were rolling down his face, and Dorothy took a tissue from her bag and handed it to him. Then, on an impulse, she kissed one of the tears and said gently.

"You poor soul."

"Not me," he croaked. "I somehow made it to shore, but fourteen of my men just drowned, and all because of me."

"Not because of you, Tim. Because of the brutal stupidity of war. I'm going to get you another pint; best bitter, wasn't it? And guess what, I'm having a gin and tonic this time, and my doctor can go forth and multiply."

By the time she returned, he was more composed, but still pale in the face.

"You OK?" she asked.

"Yes. Sorry again about all that."

"Think nothing of it; makes you more human."

"It earned me a kiss, though," he grinned. She frowned in mock severity.

"If you tell me that you only put on all that performance in order to con me out of a kiss, I really will slap your face."

"No, it was genuine enough, unfortunately. But look, what else have you learned from the dead? It helps if you keep me up-to-date with all this."

Dorothy recounted everything, from Lil's request to find Ernie, right through to Violet's phone call a couple of days previously.

Tim listened attentively, with no hint of laughter, and finally said, "I think we really do have something to investigate here. The factory records suggest that the child was Lil's, which Lil – or rather her ghost – confirmed to you, but the birth register shows the child as Bert's. I can see now why he wanted you to search the leave records. From what they taught me of military history during my training, I seem to recall that there was no leave from France in the last stages of the war, unless you were wounded, of course."

"And if the boy *was* registered as Bert's, then no wonder Lil wants Ernie to learn the truth," Dorothy added. "I'm assuming that he's still alive, of course. We also need to know what happened to Bert after the war, when he came home and found that Mabel had died, if that's how it worked out. Can you find that out for me; or is it 'us' now?"

"Definitely 'us'. The records will only show when he was discharged, which at a guess would have been shortly after the armistice, probably just before Christmas of 1918. Good job you weren't searching the birth records for 1919, by the way. The returning soldiers made up for lost time, and 1919 was a record year for births. I managed to arrive five years ahead of the boom, in 1914."

"Me too," Dorothy confirmed. "I was born just before my father began his illustrious military career. Knowing him, he was more than likely sitting somewhere safe, drawing up sophisticated plans for getting *other* people killed."

"I would never have guessed we were the same age," Tim observed. "And that's not just idle flattery; you look years younger than fifty-four."

"The art of camouflage," Dorothy joked. "I pay an arm and a leg to my hairdresser to keep the grey out of sight, and I'm officially ash blonde."

"You're unofficially beautiful," Tim murmured under his breath.

"Enough of that," Dorothy responded. "You've got a service record to look up."

"I'll swop it for dinner at yours. Wednesday suit you?

"OK. But don't get any ideas about stopping over. Strictly dinner and business. Tell your driver that it's just round the corner from the White Lion in Bramcote; blue curtains and a willow tree in the garden; he can't miss it."

"I'll be driving myself," Tim informed her. "My driver loves to gossip, and I can't keep him sitting out there all night while I'm inside enjoying Fanny Cradock's finest. Can I bring anything?"

"Just Bert Fletcher's service record. And your gallant attitude towards ladies who live on their own. Plus a reliable watch, to tell you when it's time to leave."

"Pay attention, men. Your lives could depend upon it." Captain Bruce tried to avoid the decomposing rats as he squelched backwards and forwards down the duckboards, with just enough room for him to pass the bedraggled and defiant-looking line of Tommies waiting to receive the latest battle orders.

"Right, the latest from Battalion HQ. At 05.30 tomorrow, the usual barrage will be followed by a push over the top, and into the German front line, on a three-whistle command from the man in charge of each trench. That'll be you, Sergeant Butler. You go over the top five minutes after the front line, and the whole show starts on a green light from the reserve line, so make sure you're looking back for the flare. I'll be back there, firing the flare on the signal from Battalion HQ."

"Didn't think yer'd be wi' *us*, up at the sharp end," Bert muttered. Simmy smirked, and the captain strode down the line, through the mud, to confront the two men.

"What did you say, lance corporal?" he demanded.

"I said looks like we'll be up at the sharp end," Bert improvised. The captain glared back at him.

"Of course you'll be up at the sharp end – that's what you joined for, isn't it?"

"Yes, sir," Bert replied, eyes dead front.

It was now late April 1918, and the Allies had gradually been pushing the Hun back across the wastelands of the Somme, back through the no-man's-land which had cost so many lives over the past four years. It now looked like a moonscape, with no recognisable buildings left anywhere around them, nothing still growing in what had once been fertile fields, and only a few carcasses of what had once been farm animals, with abandoned trenches, dug-outs, shell craters and stinking corpses everywhere.

A mile or so behind them lay the remains of the once quaint village of Villiers St. Martin, its shattered old church now playing host to Battalion HQ. In front, a quarter of a mile or so to the east, lay the front line of the German trenches. Before that, between B Company and the Germans, was their own front line. They were destined to go over the top in the second wave, on the three-whistle command from their trench line, which stretched for over half a mile to the southwest. The entire operation would start with a green flare, after the routine early morning exchange of mayhem from the field guns which were the opening act of every performance in this theatre of death.

It was just after 05.00 when Simmy handed Bert a steaming mug of cocoa, and asked, "Any news o' more parcels from 'ome?"

"Why ask me? I'm only the captain's arsewipe arahnd 'ere."

It had been several weeks since the last parcels, and rumours from the rear were that the supply lorries were too busy feeding the hungry eighteen pounders with shells, or replacing the artillery horses which seemed to be the Hun's favourite target. Still, it was good to have something to talk about in this nervous time before half their mates would get blown to kingdom come, and Bert remembered a joke he'd been told by the driver of the last lorry they'd seen this far up the line:

"So there were this young private from Shipstone's Light 'orse, who were just a simple country boy wi' no experience o' war. When the fust shells cum in at 'im, 'e panicked, an' ran like fuck back

through the lines, further an' further away from danger till 'e finally
collapsed, proper knackered, inter a ditch. 'e were just gerrin' 'is
breath back when 'e looked up, an' there on the edge o' the ditch were
a pair o' brahn shoes.

  'Forgive me sergeant!' 'e sez, 'I'm just a country boy from a
farm in Clifton, an' it were mi fust experience o' gunfire!'

  'Get up, you snivelling little runt,' sez the man in the brahn
shoes, all posh, like. 'And I'm not a sergeant, I'm an officer!'

  'Fuck me,' sez the private, ' 'ave I run that far?' ' "

Both men were still laughing when there was the faint
sound of a rattle from the enemy trenches, followed by the
ground-trembling roar of heavy artillery. Bert and Simmy
instinctively ducked, and within seconds men were rousing
themselves from sleep, and gathering from all parts of the
trench onto the duckboards beneath the ladders that led over
the top. Some of them were still pulling on clothing, some of
them were still shouldering their rifles, and some of them had
stopped to urinate on the inside of the trench wall.

After a few minutes, during which all the men kept as
flat to the enemy-side inner wall of the trench as they could,
Private Josephs called out.

"Is is just me, or are them bastards firin' way ovver ar
'eads?"

He was technically correct. This latest wave of murderous
incoming ordinance was not directed at the trench lines, but
at the tactical lines to their rear, and in particular the village
church, which was a convenient target for the German
rangefinders even without the spire which had been blown off
eighteen months previously, and which German Intelligence
had told their gunners was some sort of headquarters. They
stood there, spellbound, as the pale dawn drew up in the east
through the smoke haze.

When everyone agreed it was after 05.30, they began
listening intently, in case they missed the sound of the signal

whistles coming down the line. Even when the artillery fire stopped, leaving an eerie silence in which not even the birds sang – mainly because there were none – there was still no suggestion of the whistles which would send them up the ladders and out of the trenches, to face almost certain death yet again.

"Sarge?" Bert asked nervously, "what's 'appened ter the green flare?"

"Fucked if I know," the sergeant replied, keeping his eyes glued back towards the rear line. "I can't blow mi whistle till we gets the signal, then five minutes after the front line goes in. Yer'll just 'ave ter wait."

"It's all right," Simmy joked lamely, "there'll be another one be'ind."

Fifteen minutes later, Sergeant Butler was seriously concerned.

"Summat or other must 'ave 'appened ter the captain. Fletch, Simmy; get back there an' find aht what's what."

Bert and Claude shouldered their rifles and ran up the communications trench between the second and reserve lines, which the Germans had obligingly dug for them before retreating a week earlier. When they reached the reserve line, they paused for breath and enquired after Captain Bruce.

"I ain't seen 'im," they were advised by a corporal from the Wessex Regiment.

" 'e were s'posed ter be firin' a flare fer the line attack from somewhere in 'ere," Bert explained between wheezes.

"Well, 'e ain't 'ere, *izee*?" came the reply.

"Nah what?" Simmy asked Bert. Bert looked back towards the church.

" 'e said the signal'd cum from up there in Battalion HQ. Better go an' ask *them*. Mebbe the captain were killed or summat."

They left the trench and joined the pitted roadway with its many shell holes. As they were approaching the church, Bert stopped and was looking intently at the front window of what appeared to have been an inn next to the shattered signpost which had once welcomed visitors into Villiers St. Martin.

"Wharrisit, Fletch?" Simmy asked.

"Dunno, burrit looked like an officer in uniform. Mebbe we should ask in there, rather than lookin' like a pair o' fuckin' idiots when we speaks ter the top brass in the church."

Bert walked across the road, and opened the front door of the inn, which was partly hanging from its hinges anyway. Simmy heard him ask, "What the fuck a' *you* doin' in 'ere?" before a shot rang out. Ten seconds later, Captain Bruce appeared in the doorway, hanging on to the doorframe and pointing his pistol.

Private Claude Simpson froze to attention, and waited for the shot that never came.

CHAPTER SEVEN

Roast pork with extra mystery

Dorothy pulled down the oven door, partly to check that the roast was browning nicely, and partly to allow the delicious aroma to welcome Tim into the house. Then she closed it again, moved through to her front room and waited at the window until a green MG sports car appeared round the corner from Town Street and slowed down as it pulled up outside. The driver's door opened and Tim emerged, leaning on his cane as he limped round to the pavement and opened the garden gate. He waved with his cane when he saw her standing there between the curtains, and she waved back, cursing under her breath at her naivety. There was no point in pretending now, so she threw open the front door, and gave him a chaste kiss on the cheek before stepping back to let him in.

"Something smells good!" he enthused, as he handed her two bottles wrapped in tissue paper. "Didn't know if red or white was appropriate, so I brought one of each. They're cheaper in the mess."

"Can you arrange for me to do my shopping there?" she asked. He laughed lightly.

"You might need an extra bottle when you hear what I've got to tell you. You've solved one mystery and uncovered another, it seems."

"What do you mean?"

"Can we have a drink first? And then perhaps some of that delicious roast?"

"How do you know it's a roast?"

"My mother was an excellent cook. No doubt her Italian

background. Mine's a whisky and soda, if you've got one."

"The soda's Fine Fare's, I'm afraid, and I'll have mine with lime."

"I thought you were a gin and tonic girl."

"Only on Saturdays. Anyway, come through and sit down."

She carefully poured him a whisky and soda under his direction, and handed him the finely cut Lismore glass before pouring herself a soda and lime, and joining him on the sofa.

"So what did you find out?"

"You were right; or, rather, *we* were right. Lance Corporal Herbert Fletcher had no leave after 1916. In fact, he never came back here at all."

"Killed in action?"

"Shot for cowardice."

He allowed her to digest that bit of news, and when the shock had left her face he began to explain, as he pulled a few stapled sheets from the inside pocket of his tweed jacket and placed them on the coffee table between them.

"Unfortunately, so-called 'cowardice' was not unusual in the World War One trenches. Those poor buggers had it ten times worse than we ever did in the second show. They were under twenty-four-hour threat of a shell landing in their laps, and they were gassed almost daily. They lived up to their knees in mud, rats, dead bodies and God knows what else, and towards the end they couldn't even sleep under cover. Most of them had dysentery, trench foot, ulcers, lice, body sores ..."

"Yes, I get the picture," Dorothy interrupted him with a shudder.

"Sorry. Well, anyway, apart from all that, they were constantly fighting the enemy, and must have been half-deafened by the noise of shells exploding. Almost every day it was 'over the top' with fixed bayonets, and if *you* didn't get yours in first, you could expect one in your ... "

"You're enjoying this, aren't you?" Dorothy interrupted

again, accusingly.

"Far from it, believe me. My point is that many cases of alleged cowardice were just some poor bastard temporarily cracking up when his system couldn't take any more. Look how you've reacted, just by being made to imagine it! On top of all that, they were half-starved, drinking polluted water, sometimes not hearing from home for weeks on end. No wonder they occasionally lost it and ran screaming out of the trench – which would probably get them shot by an enemy sniper anyway – or diving into a funk hole and crying for their mothers."

"Tim, please get on with it – this is really upsetting me!"

"Well, to get to the nub of all this, there was an obvious need to keep morale as high as it could be cranked, and the way chosen by the top brass of the British Expeditionary Force was to make the men more scared of the consequences of running away than they were of facing the Hun one more time. Ergo, cowardice was made a court-martial offence, and death by firing squad was the automatic penalty if found guilty."

"So Bert was court-martialled?"

"No, that's the curious thing. He was shot by an officer, almost a mile back from the front line. It wasn't unheard of for this to happen during actual combat, but it normally required a full report from all available witnesses, in order to justify the officer's action."

"So what did the report on Bert say?"

"There wasn't one."

"What?"

"According to the service record Bert was shot by a captain . . . " Tim paused and flipped over a page, " . . . ah, here we are, a Captain Gordon Bruce, MacLaren Highlanders. Things were so complicated by that stage of the war that entire companies of the original infantry regiments had been wiped out, or what was left of them had been merged with other regiments, and so on. By 1918, what was left of the Robin

Hoods could be found all over Flanders, and Bert's battalion had merged with others, and had Scottish officers drafted in after their regiments had been all but decimated."

"Sounds like a record-keeper's nightmare."

"Exactly. Which is probably why no-one bothered to dig deeper into Bert's demise. The only other witness was a private in the Robin Hoods who claimed to have nothing to say."

"So, apart from this dodgy witness, for all we know this Captain Whatshisface was able to settle an old score with Bert, and get clean away with it."

"That's one interpretation. But we have to ask ourselves, why was Bert so far back from the front line if he wasn't running away?"

"Who knows? Do we know if he was supposed to be in the front line?"

"Impossible to say after all this time, I'm afraid."

There was a buzzing ring from the oven in the kitchen, and Dorothy rose to her feet slightly too quickly, and winced.

"You OK?" Tim asked, a sympathetic look on his face.

"Yes, just a touch of arthritis. Nothing to what those poor bastards had to put up with, as you reminded me. Anyway, the dinner's ready. Roast pork. Hope you're not Jewish. Oh no, Italian, wasn't it?"

"Half Italian. Would you like me to carve?"

"Thanks, but I need more practice with the new-fangled electric carving knife that my soppy sister bought me two Christmases ago. She knows I don't do much entertaining, but she has a thing about all the latest gadgets."

Dorothy went into the kitchen and lifted out the roast, then connected the carving knife to the power point above the draining board.

"It comes with all the trimmings. Is that OK?" she shouted to the other room.

"Si," he shouted back.

"Grazzi," she yelled, not to be outdone. "Do you like

crackling?"

"I don't know – I've never crackled," he joked back from the kitchen doorway. She turned round and frowned.

"And what about stuffing?"

"I'd prefer not to answer that!"

"Please go back in there and sit down at the table near the front window. And there are no waitresses you can trip up, so sit where you like."

"Red or white?"

"Which do you recommend?"

"The white would be more appropriate – it's a nice Semillon Blanc. But my genes tell me to drink the Valpollicella."

"Better open them both, then."

Once she had served up the roast and they had helped themselves to vegetables, she was curious to learn more about his background.

"So tell me about your Italian mother."

"Giovanna Zorda, but everyone called her Gina. She was big, dark-haired and beautiful. And, as I said, a wonderful cook. My father met her in Genoa, where she was working as a waitress, and he was completing what must have been one of the last grand tours ever conducted by an English gentleman. That was in 1908, and they were married precisely nine months before I was born."

"Brothers and sisters?"

"A younger brother, Robert – 'Roberto' as mum insisted on calling him. He was shot down over Dresden, flying a Lancaster."

"Sorry."

"Not as much as he was, I suppose. But now it's your turn."

Dorothy grimaced. "Born to an army officer and his timid bride of seventeen. He was called Ernest, but then so was just about everyone else back then, it seems; apart from the girls, of course. Which brings me back to *our* Ernie. He might have been raised believing his father was a coward."

"Possibly; it was a serious matter in those days. But you're not getting off that easily."

"Sorry. I was born just outside London, because that's where daddy was based in those days. We moved to Cambridge after the war, when he got himself a cushy number at the university, teaching 'strategic studies' as it was called. Some sort of intelligence stuff, from what I could deduce. My soppy sister, Edith, was two years older than me, and really took to life in the Fens, which is more than could be said for me. I left home as soon as I could, which I regret now, looking back on it. My mum, Eleanor, was a gem, and she died while I was pretending to do research in a lab in Chiswick. By that time I'd got myself pregnant but managed to wangle an abortion. There you have it; some of it, anyway. You'll get the rest when we decide what to do about our mystery. In the meantime, there's coffee and cheese and biscuits. Sound OK?"

"Fine."

"But this witness to Bert's death," she enquired as she spread some Camembert onto a cracker, "I assume you've got a name for him?"

"Of course. Simpson, from memory. I can go and get those papers from the coffee table, if you insist."

"No need. Just wondering if he's still alive."

"You really don't intend to give up, do you?"

"Well, just imagine; there could be some poor sod out there who's spent all his life believing that his dad – whom he never even met – was a coward. I'd like to be the one to tell him that he wasn't, if that's the case."

"And while you're at it, I expect you want to tell him who his real father was?"

"Wouldn't *that* be nice! Can it be done?"

"How the blazes do *I* know? First things first, though. I'll see what I can get on Private Simpson, in return for the rest of your life story."

"Why do I feel like a hostage being interrogated? OK, here it is. I married straight out of the WAAF, to a dumb-arsed former Spitfire pilot who thought he was going to be a top actor. He finished up a first-class queer and got himself a jail term for importuning in a public lavatory. So I flushed him down the same toilet, after suffering a nervous breakdown from all the embarrassment. That was in 1950. A year after that, it was the turn of an architect I met on holiday in Greece. His erections were in the neo-classical style, and frequent, but not always with me. He gave me my daughter – Sophie – and then he gave his office assistant a boy, and cleared off. The rotten shit also reported me to the authorities when he didn't get custody of Sophie. Claimed, with total accuracy, that I was an alcoholic living with an Italian painter in Ealing. Sophie was taken off me and I had another nervous breakdown to go with the first. So, ergo, to use your favourite phrase, I have a potential alcohol problem, I'm under a shrink for my nerves, and I got arthritis when the lousy stinking wop pushed me down a flight of stairs because I wouldn't give him a child. I got a fractured hip, and he got nine months."

"I see now where you got your Italian from."

"Trust me, I can swear in Italian to make any Venetian gondolier blush. But now, I believe I can claim the prize of hearing you tell me that you're going to search for Private Simpson."

He looked down at his wrist.

"My reliable wristwatch tells me that it's almost eleven o'clock. Don't know about you, but I've got to be up early in the morning. You have a choice of the Cadland on Saturday, or the Officers' Mess on Monday, when it's Ladies' Night. Your move."

"Would you class me as a lady, after what I just told you about myself?"

"I'd class you as one of the most attractive ladies I've ever met, who's hurting so much that I just want to hold her in my arms and make it all better. But since I'm so gallant, I'll just say thank you for a lovely evening, toodle-pip, and see you on Monday. My driver will pick you up at six-thirty."

He left fairly briskly, and she was able to wave him a cheery farewell and lock the door firmly behind him before the tears came.

At number seventy, they managed the whole business very effectively. Lil went into labour late on Saturday afternoon. Mabel was working days that week, and by the time she arrived home Lil's waters had just broken and Vera was beginning to panic. Mabel immediately slipped out of the house and down the road to fetch the midwife. She had the story ready prepared, which was perhaps as well.

The front door opened to reveal a dowdy-looking woman with the short stub of a cigarette hanging out of the corner of her mouth.

"Nurse Cowan? I'm Lillian Jenkins; yer've already bin asked ter attend Mabel Fletcher, at seventy New Tythe Street. Well, she's gone inter labour. Can yer cum wi' me *nah*? Only I don't know what ter do, never 'avin' 'ad any o' mi own, like. I'm ter tell yer that 'er waters broke 'alf an 'our since."

"Yeah, I'm Mary Cowan, but I were told the woman at seventy's meant ter be *you*."

"Me? Do I look pregnant?"

"Course yer don't. But the doctor said it were a Lillian Jenkins what's expectin'."

"Doctor Plowright, up in Station Road?"

"Yeah."

"Nar! It were me what asked 'im ter arrange fer yer ter cum ter Mabel when she were due. She were a bit wacked that week so I went rahnd ter the doctor's instead of 'er. The stupid bogger musta gorrus names mixed up."

"Aye, an' it wouldn't be the fust time, neither. Wait there while I get mi bag an' change mi clothes."

Back at the house, Lil gave a first-class performance as Mabel, although most of her efforts were directed at delivering a healthy eight-pound boy after a seven-hour labour. The midwife came down the stairs to find Vera dusting the mantelpiece, from which she had carefully removed Mabel and Bert's wedding photograph, as instructed by Mabel. Ethel had been safely shipped off for a few days' holiday with Uncle Joe.

Vera nodded her way through the midwife's congratulations upon becoming a granny, and made a pot of tea. Just before she left, the midwife reminded them to register the birth.

"Nah don't forget, yer must go dahn ter the Register Office wi'in forty-two days."

"Can anyone do it?" Mabel enquired innocently.

"It's usually the mam or dad what does it. 'er upstairs, o' course, but she's gunner need a day or two in bed fust, after all she's bin through. Burrit could be someone else who were 'ere at the birth. You could do it, or the prahd grandmother 'ere."

"Aye all right, we'll see ter it," Mabel assured her, as she showed her the door.

Mabel walked round to the Register Office in the High Street on the Monday morning, and listened patiently while the old man behind the counter warned her of all the terrible things that could happen to her if she told a lie, then gave him all the appropriate details and formally registered the birth of her new son, Ernest Fletcher.

Then it was back home with a triumphant grin, and the pleasure of handing the brand new birth certificate to Vera, with instructions to "tell Sam ter stick this up 'is arse" before she caught the late afternoon train to work, where she passed on the good news to all Lil's friends and workmates.

Ernest Fletcher had entered the world five days after his

official father was officially shot for cowardice.

"The chef recommends the Beef Wellington, madam."

Dorothy smiled up at the uniformed steward. "I've only ever had that once before, and it was delicious. I'll have that, please."

"And for you, sir?" he asked Tim.

"The sirloin, please – medium rare. And a bottle of the Anjou Rosé."

"Very good, sir, madam."

As he oozed back towards the kitchen, Dorothy asked, "Did you manage to get the information on Mr Stinson?"

"*Simpson*," he corrected her. "Claude Simpson. And yes I did, but it was one of those amazing coincidences which make you believe that fate's on your side."

"Why, what happened?"

"Well, the records are all kept in London, at the Public Record Office. The same person who gave me the gen on Bert was also able to tell me that Private Claude Simpson was discharged with an honourable mention in January of 1919. That should have been the end of it, but as luck would have it, there was a written request on the file for confirmation of his wartime service, and in particular the fact that he'd been mustard gassed in 1915, when he applied for a place in an ex-servicemen's assisted housing complex near Ollerton only last year. London gave me the address, I telephoned them, and ..."

"Ergo," Dorothy chipped in.

"Yes, ergo, I've got his address."

"Splendid! At least we know *he's* still alive. When are you free to go?"

"Me? Why me?"

"Because first of all, you know where it is; secondly, I don't trust my old A40 to make it all the way to Ollerton;

thirdly you have access to a car and driver, and finally, and most importantly, if you wear your uniform and arrive in an official-looking car, he'll be more inclined to tell the truth."

"I admire your faith in all but your A40. But my driver'll not be pleased to be called out on a weekend. He can be a bit difficult sometimes."

"He seemed charming enough to me when he brought me down here this evening, and he said what a pleasure it would be to drive me home later."

"That might have something to do with the short skirt you're wearing, not to mention the blouse which needs some work on the top button."

Dorothy's hand flew down to just below her throat, then she grinned at Tim. "Got me there, you bugger! I'd not got you down as a practical joker."

He grinned back. "What say we go up in my car?"

"Thank you for conceding that you'll be coming with me, but I couldn't sit for an hour and a half in your little green coffin without aggravating my arthritis."

"Leave it with me, anyway. I'll pick you up at nine on Saturday, one way or the other."

It had been a difficult night, and George Smedley's ulcer had been playing up again, so Mabel was looking forward to a nice cup of tea, a couple of slices of toast and jam, and then bed. She let herself in, and sensed immediately that something was different. Sam's cap was still on the hook behind the front door, and she could hear the kettle singing on the hob. If Sam hadn't gone to work, why was Vera up this early? She walked through to the living room, and there sat Lil, a piece of paper on the dining table in front of her, and her eyes red-raw with crying.

"What're *you* doin' up?" Mabel asked. "Is summat up wi'

Ernie?"

"No, Ernie's fine. But yer needs ter sit dahn, mi duck."

"Wharrisit?"

Mabel put her bag down on the floor, and sat down. Lil slid the small piece of paper across the table to her, and got up to go and make the tea. Mabel read the paper, and at first didn't take it in. Then she read it again, and still didn't believe it. Then she let out an animal scream and fainted.

She came round to find Vera and Lil fussing over her, and laying her out more comfortably on the floor. She scrambled to her feet, grabbed the telegram and read it once more, in case it had all been a bad dream. But it hadn't.

REGRET TO ADVISE LANCE CORPORAL HERBERT FLETCHER KILLED IN ACTION TWENTY-NINTH APRIL. DEEPEST CONDOLENCES. LETTER TO FOLLOW.

As Mabel's tears splashed down on the buff form, Lil put her arm around her and squeezed.

"It's a kick in the bleedin' teeth, mi gel, but we 'as ter get through it. Lots o' women 'ave bin through it before."

"But why my Bert?" Mabel wailed.

"It musta bin 'is turn," came Sam's voice from the staircase. Lil rushed to meet him, and whispered hoarsely in his face.

"You say owt ter upset 'er right nah, an' I'll kick yer balls off! Nah be'ave yerself fer once!"

" 'e were my son an' all, yer know," Sam reminded her, and for the first time Lil saw a tear in his eye. He walked up to Mabel and hugged her tightly as they both cried helplessly.

"I'll mek the tea," Vera said, through tears of her own.

———◈———

"It's ironic, when you think about it," Tim observed as they sped through the avenues of birch trees on the road out of Edwinstowe, "they were called the Robin Hoods, and here we are in Sherwood Forest."

He had borrowed a pool car for the day, but the shiny new leather-upholstered Rover seemed somewhat out of place amidst the ancient glades where Robin and his Merry Men used to play hide and seek with the Sheriff of Nottingham. Dorothy lowered her sunglasses and looked again at the directions which Tim had written down.

"Your handwriting could do with improvement," she commented.

"I thought even schoolteachers had a day off occasionally. In any case, you're supposed to be navigating, not marking my essay."

"According to this childlike scrawl, we turn left at something called 'Robin's Lair'. Not sure if that's a pub or a local landmark."

"We'll find out soon enough," Tim told her. "Here's the turn-off."

Five minutes later, they parked the car in the visitors' car park and went in search of number twenty-three. They were just approaching its front gate when a woman in a nurse's uniform closed the front door behind her and began to walk down the path. They met at the gate, and she looked at them enquiringly.

"Are you here to see Mr Simpson?" she asked, glancing at Tim's uniform. "Is it to do with his pension?"

"No, it's just a personal visit."

"Didn't know he had any family left. But please remember not to upset him. He's only just had his tablet, and his emphysema's not going to improve if he gets upset."

"Don't worry," Dorothy smiled encouragingly, "I'm sure he'll be glad to see us."

If he was glad to see them, it didn't register on his face as he opened the front door and noticed Tim's uniform.

"Is it summat ter do wi' mi 'ousin'?" he enquired nervously.

"No, nothing to do with that. We just want you to tell us something about your experiences in the trenches."

"Yer'd best cum in, then. Would yer like a cuppa? I've just mashed, as it 'appens."

A cup of tea and two arrowroot biscuits later, Tim got down to business.

"You were in the Robin Hoods in that last push across the Somme, weren't you?"

"Aye," Claude conceded guardedly.

"And you had a comrade in arms called Bert Fletcher. He was your lance corporal, I believe?"

Claude's previously open expression slammed shut.

"I told 'em all I knew back then. Yer'll get nowt ahter me!"

Dorothy tried a different approach.

"We've been looking at the army records, and it may be that Bert was falsely accused of cowardice."

"Not bi me 'e weren't."

"No, but he was shot by an officer a mile back from the front line," Tim reminded him. "Can you tell us why he was back there in the first place?"

" 'e were sent back, bi the sergeant. Me an' 'im."

"You were *with* him?" Dorothy asked.

"Course I were! Don't it say so in the papers?"

"Not directly," Tim informed him. "The papers just say that you witnessed the shooting."

"Aye, that's right. That bleedin' officer – a Scotch bloke – 'e 'ad a downer on Bert fer weeks, an' when we fahnd 'im in that pub, 'e shot Bert an' told me ter fuck off or 'e'd shoot me an' all. Oh, sorry, miss."

"Don't worry. I heard far worse than that from officers in RAF control rooms during the last war," Dorothy assured him.

"You found the officer in a *pub*?" Tim persevered.

"Well, they didn't call 'em pubs ovver there, did they? Burrit 'ad bin a pub or summat before the Germans shelled it. 'e were in there, the officer tharris, an' 'e were *drunk*! We'd bin sent ter find 'im, 'cos 'e 'adn't fired the flare 'e were supposed ter shoot off ter start the attack. We was bein' shelled summat rotten bi Fritz, an' we thought 'e might be dead, so the sergeant sent us back dahn the line ter Battalion HQ ter find aht what were what. We fahnd the pub just before the church where we was 'eadin', an' we fahnd 'im in it, an' 'e shot Bert an' threatened ter do the same ter me."

"What did you tell the commanding officer at the time?"

"Same as wharra told you just nah. I were told ter keep mi gob shut, an' say nowt. The next day we 'eard as the officer'd bin sent back dahn the line, an' we went ovver the top an' never stopped chasin' Fritz till the Germans surrendered. November, that were."

"Did you know that Bert was listed as a coward?" Dorothy asked.

"Bert weren't no coward!" Claude insisted. "The officer what shot 'im were the coward!"

"Thank you so much!" Dorothy said, as she reached across the table and squeezed his hand.

"Are you 'is family?" Claude asked.

"No," Dorothy replied. "Let's just say that we're friends of the family."

Claude looked apprehensively at Tim.

"Will this affect mi pension?"

"Not at all," Tim reassured him. "You brave men deserve every ha'penny the Government gives you. If it hadn't been for your courage, we wouldn't be sitting here now. Thank you for being so frank with us, and God bless you."

The old man wiped a tear from his cheek, and showed them to the door, wheezing every step of the way.

They were back in the car, and on the way home, when

Dorothy asked, "God bless you? Do you believe in God?"

"Not really, but *he* does. Didn't you see the plaster icon on the wall? Christ on the cross?"

"Can't say I did. I was too interested in what he had to say. Why would the authorities allow Bert to die a coward's death, when he'd only been obeying orders?"

"Morale for one thing, like I explained already. Plus, a cover-up for a drunken officer, and the only witness scared out of his wits that the same would happen to him."

"That's a disgrace! The family lived with that shame unnecessarily for the rest of their lives. It's now even more important that we find the son and tell him what we've just learned. I only hope he'll believe us."

"I can do better than that," Tim said as his knuckles went white on the steering wheel. "I'm going to apply to have the entire business reinvestigated, and the record cleared. Bert can't have been the only poor bastard that happened to, and there has to be accountability!"

"Go get 'em, Robin!" Dorothy quipped. "And the next pub we come to, it's my treat for the ploughman's."

CHAPTER EIGHT

The Nit Parade

Lil was back at work by the first week in June, but on the opposite shift to Mabel, as agreed before the birth. This way, there was always someone there to look after Ethel and Ernie, without any need to burden Sam and Vera.

Lil had been allowed to stay on with the Fletchers, after pleading with Sam not to send her back to her mother. Ada Jenkins had only once looked in to see her grandson, and then only after a threat from Mabel that she would see no more money – from either her or Lil – if she did not. Once she was back on her feet, Lil visited her mother with Ernie every Sunday afternoon, but as the weeks went by, her visits got shorter and shorter. Ada was never told that Ernie had been registered as Bert and Mabel's child, and for the first two weeks after his birth, Mabel was paid the extra two shillings a week. Then the entire pension stopped, once some army payroll clerk realised that Bert was dead.

A week or so after the telegram, while Mabel was at work, there was a visit from a very sympathetic lady called Polly Morgan, who explained that she was representing the local War Pensions Committee. Lil had listened very carefully to the conversation between Polly and the Fletchers, and was able to tell Mabel, in the short time they had together in the changing rooms during the shift change, that she would probably be entitled to a widow's pension in respect of Bert's death, with a possible extra two and sixpence a week each for Ethel and Ernie. Then, the following week, the next blow fell when the letter arrived from Regimental Field Headquarters.

"I don't believe it!" Mabel shouted, close to tears. "My Bert a coward? *Never*!"

"Well, that's what the lerrer sez," Sam snapped irritably. "An' I 'spect that's put paid ter yer widder's pension an' all."

"Never mind the pension fer nah, Sam," Vera intervened. "Read me the lerrer again, Mabel."

Almost choking on the words, Mabel reread out loud what was meant to be the comforting letter from the Commanding Officer of the 1ˢᵗ Battalion of the Sherwood Foresters, who had written to break the news that Bert had been shot by the officer in command of his company when he caught him attempting to flee the front line during heavy artillery bombardment. Although it was a matter of considerable regret that it had been essential to morale for the officer to take this action, and for Bert's service record to end with the words 'cowardice in the face of the enemy', the reports from his various company commanders in the past suggested that he had otherwise been a brave and gallant soldier, whose tragic demise must, like so many during this conflict, be put down as one of the tragedies of war.

" 'e sez it 'imself!" Mabel protested. "My Bert went through four years o' shit, an' never once turned 'is back on 'is duty. 'e were even given a stripe. I'll *never* believe 'e were a coward. It's bad enough tharris dead, but why does they 'ave ter rub it in an' call 'im a coward? 'e were the best man I ever knew!"

She hunched up over the dining table at which she had been sitting, and screwed the letter into a tight ball before throwing it across the room and screaming. Vera put her arms around her, but Mabel shrugged her off and raced up to the bedroom, where her racking sobs could be heard for fully half an hour. Then, after what had been a tiring night shift only hours earlier, she seemed to pass out on the bed, and Vera left her alone after covering her up with a blanket where she lay, fully clothed, on top of the sheets.

The noise had awoken Ernie, who began crying for food. Vera decided that Mabel needed all the sleep she could get, so she took the baby downstairs wrapped in a shawl, and began to mix his feed. Ethel sat quietly in the corner, playing morosely with a doll which Uncle Joe had bought her on a recent trip to Nottingham. Eventually, Sam was prepared to keep quiet no longer.

"Well, we've gorrarsens lumbered wi' *two* kids, nah. Bad enough ter 'ave Ethel ovver there, but since Mabel were persuaded ter claim fer 'im an' all . . ."

"It were *you* what did the persuadin', once yer thought yer could mek money aht on it!" Vera protested.

"Be that as it may, Lil's gunner 'ave ter tek responsibility fer the little bastard; 'e can't live 'ere forever."

"Mebbe 'er mam'll cum rahnd eventually, but if she does we'll not 'ave Lil's money comin' in, neither."

"Aye, yer right there. Mind yer, she giz most've it ter the old cow as it is. All I'm sayin' is that summat else'll 'ave ter be done wi' Ernie."

"So what d'yer suggest?" Vera demanded. "Go an' tell the authorities that we told lies abaht 'im in the fust place? You 'eard what Mabel said abaht goin' ter prison fer lyin' abaht what goes in them records dahn the registry."

"That were 'er, not me," Sam objected.

"You were part've it an' all, remember. Yer was glad enough ter tek the fust money what cum in from Bert's army pay, an' yer sat there an' told that there welfare woman as 'ow Ernie were ar Bert's kid. Yer not gerrinaht've it that easy, Sam Fletcher."

Sam grumbled under his breath, but let it drop – for the time being.

Standing in New Tythe Street, Dorothy gazed disconsolately

at the scene before her, then checked the numbers again. The terrace of late Victorian houses definitely ended at number sixty-six, and where number seventy should have been was a piece of waste ground, and beyond that a fairly substantial detached villa. She'd had little enough hope of tracing Ernie Fletcher through the people who might still have been living in the old house, but even that remote prospect now had to be discounted.

She got back in her car to return home. Turning into Station Road, she joined a long queue of traffic heading towards the busy Nottingham Road, and glanced idly across at the shop window to her left, which was some sort of tailor's shop advertising 'Return To School' uniforms. She was reminded that her long summer break was almost over, and that in two weeks or so she'd be back trying to instil the basics of science into acne-ridden numbskulls. No wonder they used to call the feeder schools 'elementary' schools, she grinned – they were full of elementals! Suddenly, a light bulb lit up inside her head.

Once home, she phoned the school and got Christine Pullman's home number on the pretence of some timetabling problem – Christine was, after all, in charge of Senior School timetabling – and was relieved when Christine herself answered.

"Chris, it's Dorothy here. Dorothy Younger. Have you lived in Sawley all your life?"

"Not yet."

"Very funny, Chris. Seriously though, have you always lived there?"

"No," came the reply, "we moved here in sixty-five, when Ted opened that new vet clinic in Long Eaton. Before that we lived in Derby. Why?"

"I was just after some information on Long Eaton school records. I'm trying to trace a family friend who probably went to a Long Eaton elementary school in about 1920 or so. I remember you telling me that when you completed your DipEd last year, your final dissertation was on the history of education in Derbyshire, so I thought you might be able to give me some pointers."

"Well, I did make quite a few useful contacts at the time. Give me the name, and I'll see what I can do."

"You're a gem, as always, Chris. I'll bring in some Wagon Wheels for our first week's tea breaks."

"That's a point; it's only a couple of weeks away, isn't it? Why do the holidays always go so much quicker than the terms?"

"Perhaps because we enjoy them more. The name I've got is Ernest Fletcher, born the fourth of May 1918, New Tythe Street, Long Eaton. Is that enough?"

"Hang on a sec, let me write that down. OK, that should do for starters. Ted's out somewhere near Shardlow with his arm up a cow's arse, so I can probably get onto it today. What's your number there?"

The next day, Christine called back, with good news and bad news. The bad news was that there appeared to be no surviving records for any Long Eaton state elementary schools.

"But I must be well in with the man upstairs, because on a whim I called Laura Simmons, who's the school secretary at the Grammar School. She checked the records and they've got someone answering the description of your boy. I owe her one, and you owe me a year's supply of Wagon Wheels. Laura's expecting to hear from you."

Another set of profuse thanks, and then a quick call to Tim at work, to pass on the promising news. He seemed a bit down, and, worried that he might be losing enthusiasm, Dorothy invited him over for what she chose to call 'a late tea' the following evening, then called it a day.

By the time that she was lifting the quiche out of the oven, and kissing Tim on the cheek as he handed her a bottle of

Chianti, she had even more news to impart.

"I went over to the Grammar School this morning, and the very helpful secretary was able to tell me that Ernie left there in 1936 for a commercial apprenticeship with Ladywood Iron Foundries. They're still in the phone book, although they've changed their name to Euro Metals, or something equally wet. Anyway, according to them, Ernie left there at the outbreak of war in 1939, and joined the RAF. Over to you."

Tim's face clouded as he swirled the last of his whisky and soda around his glass.

"Bit of a hiccup there, I'm afraid. I got the bollocking of my life when I contacted the War Office and suggested that they might like to reopen the case of Bert Fletcher. The colonel first of all asked me – and I'll leave out all the bad language – what the blank I was playing at, and that if I didn't blankingwell stop all my blanking interfering, he'd personally ensure that I was blankingwell reprimanded. He also told me to blankingwell stop examining old blanking record files which have nothing to do with my blanking job, and are none of my blanking business."

"So you drew a blank, so to speak?" Dorothy joked over the top of her gin and tonic.

"You could say that. So when, and if, I go fishing around in old RAF files, I can expect an earlier transfer back to Bicester than I had anticipated."

Dorothy felt a little downhearted at the thought of this.

"I'd forgotten that you're only here temporarily. Seems a pity, really. We've only just met, and there's so much left to discover about Ernie, and everything."

"May I extract, from that, some hope that you don't actually want to see the back of me when my usefulness has expired?"

"Define 'usefulness'. Even though your days as a records ferret may be coming to an untimely end, I may have some other uses for you."

He leaned across without warning and kissed her on the lips. She first backed off instinctively, then came back and returned the kiss. They separated and smiled, and Dorothy decided that it was time to serve the pâté.

The most notable event in the shell factory in June 1918 was an outbreak of head lice among the workforce. Every worker, shift by shift and department by department, was ordered over to the medical room, where a piece of white paper was placed on the table in front of which they sat while a stony-faced nurse pulled a steel comb through their hair, and watched for the offending lice as they fell onto the paper.

As the result of what became known as 'The Nit Parade', Lil was told to cut her hair to a passable one inch in length, ready for inspection in a week's time. As she sat at the table on the Sunday morning, wailing and moaning at the prospect of losing the long blonde locks which she regarded as her best feature, Mabel came up with what she hoped was some sort of compensation.

"Look, gel, I'll cut yer 'air wi' them dressmakin' scissors o' Vera's, an' then yer can cut mine. Then termorrer Vera can nip dahn ter 'enshaws an' get some o' that 'air dye fer us. If we both does it at the same time, yer'll not feel so bad abaht it, 'cos I think I've gorrem an' all, what wi' sharin' a bed wi' you."

"Yer sure?" Lil enquired through the smudges in her make-up. "If yer serious, I can g'dahn ter mam's before dinner, then we can cut us 'air this afternoon."

"Course I'm serious. An' they reckon that new bob-look's all the thing nah, anyroad."

It was the following Sunday before the job was complete, and for the whole of the intervening week Lil complained about "lookin' like a walkin' bleedin' lavatory brush" and was glad that she was on nights and didn't have to walk down the street in broad daylight. However, she cheered up when the two of them applied the dye, rinsed it out, brushed their hair into what came as close as they could get to the bob-look, and admired themselves in the mirror above the mantelpiece. They both had the same dark-red mops, "lookin' like a pair o' bloody chrysanthemums" as Sam put it.

They also got a cheap giggle at Sam's expense when he came home from work a few days later and saw someone bending over the scullery sink washing dishes, and said, "I thought yer was on days this week, Lil."

"So she is," Mabel answered with a grin as she straightened up and turned round. "Don't go tellin' Lil as yer mistook me fer 'er; she still ain't recovered yet from 'avin' 'er 'air cut."

Dorothy quietly cursed the ringing phone as she sat at the dining table, preparing her teaching plan for next term's fifth form chemistry. She got carefully to her feet and lifted the handset from the cradle.

"Yes?"

"You sound a bit grumpy," Tim remarked from the other end.

"Sorry, you caught me at a bad moment, that's all. Got any news for me?"

"Yes, I'm fine, thank you for asking. But enough of this pleasant badinage. Just phoning to tell you to expect a parcel by special delivery, probably tomorrow, direct from the Public Record Office and addressed to you personally. Hope you didn't have any urgent plans for tomorrow?"

"Apart from morning coffee with the Pope, lunch with the Beatles and dinner with Omar Sharif, no."

"Excellent. OK if I nip round when it's delivered? Only those record thingies can take a bit of working through. I'll bring some Chinese in with me, if Omar likes Chinese."

"I wouldn't know, but I do. Hope it goes well with Angel Delight."

"I normally eat it with rice, but I'm always open to a new challenge."

"You might regret saying that, one day."

"Promises, promises. Tomorrow at seven then. Looking forward to it."

The phone was put down before she could think of a suitable retort. Fifth form chemistry would now have to wait while she relieved Fine Fare of one of their Angel Delights.

"I think Moselle goes with Chinese," he said, as he handed her a brown paper bag, damp with condensation, plus a larger, warmer, one which smelt deliciously of Peking Duck. "Did the parcel arrive?"

"Over there, on the coffee table. I haven't opened it yet, and I trust it didn't cost you your career."

"No, only my first-born."

"Didn't know you had kids."

"I don't. I had to promise the lady at the Public Record Office I'd give *her* first option. Don't worry, I knew her in Aldershot yonks ago and she's got a face like the north end of a south-bound hippopotamus."

"Very gallant."

"Yes, whisky and soda, thanks. Now, let's see what the Gods have in store."

He opened the parcel, removed the several sheets of photocopied paper, and muttered something that Dorothy opted not to hear.

"Problems?"

"Not really; just that Pilot Officer Ernest Fletcher seems to have maintained the family tradition."

"Not shot for cowardice, surely?"

"They didn't shoot Lancaster crews, they just left that to the Luftwaffe."

"What, then?"

"What they called LMF. Stands for 'Lack of Moral Fibre'. We used to call it a blue funk."

"And is that something you can inherit?"

"No idea. But what a supreme irony. He grew up, presumably, believing that his father was a coward, then he funked it when his turn came."

"So what happened to him?" asked Dorothy, impatiently. "He is still alive, isn't he?"

"Invalided out in 1943. Total nervous breakdown, reading between the lines. He was sent to Amhurst."

"Is that like being sent to Coventry?"

"Worse. Amhurst was, and maybe still is, a hospital for nervous wreck victims of war. At least they'll have kept decent records, and he may still be there."

"You ready for Chinese?"

"Not really, and right now I could drink that entire bottle of wine without any of it touching the sides; but let's eat, anyway."

As they sat eating in silence, Dorothy reached out her hand and held Tim's.

"Look, if this is getting too close to home for you, with your brother and everything . . ."

He smiled weakly across at her.

"No, nothing like that. It's just so bloody depressing, that's all. Let's hope things start getting more cheerful soon; *something* good's got to come out of all this."

"I think it already has. But just for the moment, Tim, you'll have to leave your overnight bag at home."

CHAPTER NINE
A bang to end all bangs

"Where exactly is Eastwood, then?" Tim enquired.

"I'll tell you that when you tell me why we're eating lunch in an Ilkeston pub."

"I've got a meeting here this afternoon," he replied evasively, "and I'm supposed to be leaving military records alone while I'm at work, *ergo* I only do it in my meal breaks."

"Fair enough. Well, by coincidence Eastwood is only a few miles east of here, on the Nottingham side of the county boundary."

Tim had come along armed with the information that Ernie had been discharged from Amhurst in 1950, into the care of his widowed sister, who had arranged for him to be taken on at the local bakery that also employed her, and that Ernie was still being paid an invalidity pension at the same address, after what appeared to have been his early retirement on health grounds.

"So we could easily get there and back in half a day?" Tim asked.

"Yes, provided that *today* is not that half-day. When we do go I want to be able to tell Ernie the whole story about his parentage; but I'm not sure how we find that out. Also, I'm not sure if he'll want a crowd there when I tell him."

"Do I look like a crowd?"

"No, but you have a military bearing about you. Ernie may have been released, or discharged, or whatever the appropriate phrase is, but he might go a bit wobbly again if he thinks that you're anything to do with the armed forces."

"I wasn't exactly planning on going in full dress uniform, with the band of the Royal Marines marching ahead of me. But you might have a point. And as far as Ernie's father is concerned, have you any idea how to find out who he really was?"

"Not a clue. Inspiration, please, in exchange for the rest of my pie. The pastry's soggy and the meat's as tough as old boots."

"You're lucky. I think the animal they used in mine must have been extinct for centuries. Another soda and lime? Or are you worried that you'll lose all your inhibitions and dance naked on the table?"

"I'd want it cleaned a little more thoroughly first. But it's my turn anyway."

When she returned with the drinks, it was clear that Tim had been thinking.

"You aren't going to like this one little bit, but there's one obvious person who could tell us – sorry, *you* – who Ernie's father was."

"The only person who fits that description is Lil herself." She looked across the table, then stared in horror and added, "Please tell me you're joking!"

"She was keen enough to speak to you *last* time."

"Yes, and then I just thought she was a loonie. This time, if she appears, I'll probably wet myself."

"I believe we have latex underwear in the depot stores. Didn't the WAAFs wear them during the war, when they were known as officers' groundsheets or something?"

"That's a very old, a very tired, and, as far as I'm concerned, a very inaccurate myth."

"We're getting off the point. Anyway, if you go back to the churchyard – and I'll come with you, if you want – she might be able to cut a lot of corners for us."

"I thought you didn't want anything more to do with the supernatural."

"Believe me, I don't. But she's your ghost, not mine. I'm just offering to be there to hold your hand, that's all. I'll also pack some spare knickers for you."

"But can't you think of any other way to find out who Ernie's father was? Please?"

"You obviously haven't seen the personnel records from the old shell factory. There were over three thousand male employees, and he could have been any one of them. Maybe a dead one, at that."

"You're really making this easy for me, aren't you?" she remarked sarcastically. "The thought of one ghost is bad enough – what if the father turns up as well?"

"Fine by me, as long as he brings his death certificate! It's time to wrap up this whole affair and get back to a normal life."

"In some ways, I'm quite enjoying the abnormal one we're leading now. Aren't you?"

"Yes, of course. But now, I really have to go. You'll be all right to drive back, won't you?"

"Why do you think I was drinking soda and lime? I've got a pre-term staff meeting this afternoon, and I could hardly attend that hiccupping and giggling. So it's back to my trusty A40, and into the early afternoon sun."

"Do I get a kiss first?"

"In the churchyard, if you meant it about coming with me."

"It's a date. When?"

"Not sure. I'll have to think about it. I'm not totally convinced yet."

"OK. Let me know when the spirits move you."

It was the height of summer, but most of those in Mabel's train compartment on her way home on Saturday evening seemed to be coughing and sneezing. It was the end of her week on days, and she was exhausted. It was more than her usual end-of-the-week lethargy, and by the time she reached the end of the twitchel and turned into Main Street and over the level crossing, she could barely drag one foot in front of the other. Somehow she made it home, but almost immediately had to stagger down the garden to the privy for an explosive bout of diarrhoea. She turned green at the smell of the fish pie that Vera had made for tea, and rushed into the scullery to vomit into the sink. Lil came after her, and stroked her back.

"Yer not well, mi duck. Best go ter bed. I'll give Ethel 'er 'ot milk an' purrer ter bed later."

"Thanks, Lil," Mabel spluttered as she reached for a glass of water. "Ter tell yer the truth I'm not sure I can even stand fer much longer."

"There's a lot on it abaht," Vera observed from the scullery doorway. "D'yer want me ter send fer the doctor?"

"No thanks, love," Mabel said. "I reckon it were just summat I 'ad at lunchtime. The pork chop were a bit underdone, an' I've bin feelin' queasy ever since."

"Well, mind yer get a good day's rest," Sam shouted from the living room. "Yer've ter be back at work Monday night, remember. Can't go missin' a shift."

"Shurrup, Sam!" Lil yelled back. "Anyone can see she's proper poorly. Cum on, duck, tek mi arm an' I'll 'elp yer up ter bed."

By Sunday morning, Mabel was delirious, and they were running out of bowls to catch the vomit, which remained in splattered pools on the wooden bedroom floor until Lil could mop it up. Vera took over the care of the children, leaving Lil to attend to Mabel. By teatime, Mabel had fallen asleep, and as they sat round the table picking listlessly at their tinned sardines and salad, Sam voiced what they were all thinking.

"D'yer reckon Mabel'll be right enough fer 'er night shift termorrer?"

"What do *you* bloody think?" Lil retorted. "She'll not be

right fer days, bi the look of 'er. At least she's stopped spewin', but the way she's sleepin' ain't natural. If she's no berrer termorrer, best get the doctor, whether she likes it or not."

"Doctors cost money," Sam objected. "We'll just see 'ow she goes."

"It's yer own daughter-in-law lyin' up there!" Lil protested. "We don't know what's wrong wi' 'er, an' I've 'eard tell as 'ow folks is dyin' from this 'ere flu what's goin' rahnd."

"All very well fer you ter say that," Sam answered back. "She's gunner miss a few shifts, bi the look of it, so where's the money gunner cum from fer the doctor?"

"I'll work 'er bloody shift, if that's all yer worried abaht," Lil spat back. Sam looked back at her quizzically.

"D'yer reckon yer could, after workin' yer own?"

"Course I bloody could. We was working eighteen 'ours straight some time back, remember? I just 'as ter go aht o' the factory, turn rahnd an' go back in again."

"Can't yer just stay in there?" asked Vera.

"No, security's tight in there, an' if yer don't show yer token at the gate on yer way aht, they sahnds the alarm. Anyroad, I'll be dyin' fer a fag bi then."

"Burrafter all that, yer've gorrer go back in an' do another *day* shift," Sam pointed out.

"So what? If it means yer'll gerra doctor in ter see ter Mabel, it's worth it."

"Won't somebody notice?" Vera enquired.

"Mebbe, mebbe not. We all look like bloody circus clarns in them overalls an' caps, an' most o' the time we're s'posed ter wear face masks an' all. An' mind 'ow Sam mistook us fer each other that time – Mabel told me all abaht that!"

"Wharrappens if yer does get caught?" asked Sam.

"God knows. I'll prob'ly go ter prison, an' Mabel'll lose 'er job fer goin' along wi' it. But we'll worry abaht that when it 'appens. I just needs Mabel's identification disc fer clockin' in, an' I know she keeps it in 'er 'andbag on a chain. I've seen 'er tek it aht o' there often enough. But if I does this, yer get the doctor in termorrer, right?"

"I'll see ter that, gel," Vera assured her, with a warning glance across the table at Sam.

The following day was hot and sweltering, to welcome in the new month. The day shift started without a hitch, but by mid-morning the B shift workers were packing ice around the TNT hopper, out of fear that it would spontaneously combust in the heat. But this created another problem, which was ultimately to prove fatal.

Ammonium nitrate had a tendency to crystallise below thirty-two degrees centigrade, and the standing order therefore was to keep the temperature in the filling rooms above that level while the mixing process was taking place. The TNT had been artificially cooled by the packed ice, with the result that when it was mixed with the ammonium nitrate, the latter began to crystallise faster than normal. The mixing room staff noticed what was happening, and were using wooden spatulas to scrape the remaining crystals off the side of the mixing pans at the end of every mix, ladling it into spare boxes which they stored round the edges of each room. It would have been more efficient had they used metal scrapers, but the risk of explosion would then have been too great, so they had to be content with wooden implements.

By the end of the shift, Mixing Room No. 2 had run out of storage boxes. They were also too busy wondering how to safely dispose of the boxes they had filled to remember to clean the mixing pan one last time. They clocked out, leaving the pan coated in a crystallised TNT and ammonium nitrate mixture, with boxes packed full of waste crystal around the walls.

Lil was the first out of the gate, and as she gratefully sucked in the first few drags of her Woodbine, she watched carefully from behind an army vehicle parked in the entrance drive. She saw Billy Nugent hand over the entrance hut to

Tommy Gardner, then stamped out her dog-end and walked briskly back towards the gate before the bulk of A shift arrived. She waved her identification disc under Tommy's nose and handed over her cigarettes and matches.

"Thought you was on B shift," he commented as he handed her the numbered token in exchange.

"I were, burra got transferred."

"That musta bin awful sudden, then, 'cos they send me the lists every week, an' yer still dahn fer B shift. I allus tek notice o' *your* name, 'cos yer a right good looker."

"That's management fer yer, allus be'ind wi' the paperwork."

"I'm not supposed ter let yer in if yer name's norron mi list. An' I know *your* face."

"Well, yer'll just 'ave ter brek the rules fer once, won't yer?"

Tommy looked doubtful, but Lil hit on a strategy. She looked quickly behind her, and noted with relief that there was no-one else approaching the gate yet. She gave him her best smile.

"Nah, Tommy, 'owdyer know I'm not 'idin' summat in mi knickers?"

"I don't, do I?"

"S'pose I let yer check fer yerself. Will that mek it OK fer me ter go through the gate?"

Tommy went bright red and began breathing heavily. Lil pushed him back into his hut, closed the door behind them, lifted her skirts to waist level and guided his hand under the drawstring of her long cotton drawers. As his rate of breathing began to accelerate she pulled his hand out, dropped her skirts and reopened the door. Members of A shift were beginning to appear from the main road as she turned and whispered back at him.

"If yer say owt, I'll accuse yer of attackin' me. Keep yer gob shut, an' I'll do the same."

Things went according to plan until George Smedley came raging into the mixing room, his face crimson.

"In two bloody years, that's the fust time the Danger Building Officer's purrin a bad report abaht one o' mi rooms. I'll bloody strangle Tom Dakin when I sees 'im next! 'is bloody lot left all this shit dahn the sides o' the mixin' pan, an' in these bleedin' boxes. We're late startin' as it is! Mabel, Nellie, Clarrie – gerrit cleaned up. *Nah*!"

As the three girls went into action, George looked hard at Lil.

"You ain't Mabel Fletcher! Tek yer mask off, an' let's see who yer *really* is; yer could be a bloody enemy spy, fer all I know!"

Lil reluctantly lowered her face mask, and George let out a bellow of rage.

"Lil fuckin' Jenkins! What's your game then, eh?"

"Shut yer stupid gob, yer fat bastard," Lil snapped back, angrily. "Mabel's got that there flu, an' we gorrer pay fer a doctor forrer."

"Norron *my* shift, gel! The regulations is very clear abaht impersonatin' another worker. Yer fer the 'igh jump, mi gel, you an' yer pal."

He moved towards the entrance door, and Lil moved to block his way. They struggled, and George broke free. As he did so, he collided with Nellie, who had been walking towards the mixing pan with a spanner to turn the screw which held the mixing pan upright, intending to turn it through ninety degrees to facilitate cleaning.

The spanner flew out of her hand and skidded down the inside of the pan, causing a series of sparks in the crystallised residue. It was the last thing any of them ever saw.

If the Great War was 'the war to end all wars' then this had been the bang to end all bangs. The final report would identify the epicentre of the explosion as having been somewhere in the danger buildings, which included the mixing house and the two melting houses for the TNT and ammonium nitrate. The report could not be any more specific than that, because there was nothing left of any of those buildings except a few sad courses of brick, hundreds of yards of twisted metal, and miles of corrugated-iron sheeting. Nor was there anything left worth calling a police station, a fire station, a garage and a canteen. There was barely a window left on the entire site, and most of the roofs had blown off the remaining factory buildings as almost eight tons of high explosive had turned itself into a greenish-black cloud which followed the prevailing wind and began to descend on neighbouring Attenborough, where residents occupied themselves in the eerie silence which followed the initial explosion by covering their noses with wet handkerchiefs, and picking up the broken window glass from the floors of their homes.

Within minutes, the silence was broken by the agitated shouting of those rushing to the scene to try and help, the noise of vehicles being brought in to ferry the seriously injured to hospital in Nottingham, and the first tremulous rumours that there might be other explosions to follow, if the mighty TNT store went up. The fact that it didn't, and the fact that the death list didn't expand beyond the initial area of impact, owed much to the courage and foresight of those who had miraculously survived death itself, and bravely worked to preserve the lives of others, even though in many cases these heroes were badly injured themselves.

The extent of the heroism displayed resulted in a demand that the factory be awarded the Victoria Cross, and although this never officially occurred, the identity discs issued to returning workers would later have 'The VC Factory' stamped on them. Some individuals were singled out for personal recognition of their bravery. Men such as Harry Andrews, who overcame serious injuries of his own to put out two fires; Alec Clarke, John Faggle and John Cross, who remained in the badly damaged press houses for long enough to shut off all the steam valves, and William Spreadbury, who continued to man the switchboard despite suffering from acute shock.

Not forgetting the almost saintly Alison McKenzie, the daughter of a Lincolnshire vicar, who was officially on duty as the ticket girl in the surviving canteen, but who crawled between live and dangling electric cables to free victims from the tangled wreckage of the partly demolished remaining buildings. She would always insist that all she did was serve tea to the injured, but to her, as to all the others, went the Order of the British Empire from the hand of the Duke of Portland.

The highest award of all went to Arthur Bristowe, Works Manager, who received the Edward Medal (later exchanged for the George Cross) for his courage in climbing up the TNT store conveyor, in company with another worker, to prevent a further fifteen tons of TNT from going skyward.

The blast had been heard or felt in some way or another for a twenty-mile radius, and Attenborough was not the only community to suffer broken windows. Mabel stirred in her troubled sleep when she heard the loud rumble, and felt the bed move beneath her, while Sam and Vera leapt out of their chairs in the living room as the crockery on the scullery shelves rattled and jingled, and threatened to fall off.

"What were *that*?" Vera speculated.

"Dunno, but it were a bloody big un," said Sam. "Sahnded like a bomb or summat. Mebbe it's a Zeppelin raid. I reckon we should look sharp an' go an' 'ide under the stairs."

Thirty minutes later, they were aware of excited voices in the street, and as they walked out to join their neighbours, one of them asked after Mabel.

"She's in bed poorly, why?" Vera enquired.

"It were 'er factory what went up. Didn't yer 'ear the bang a while ago?"

"Bloody 'ell. Lil!" Vera cried out, a hand to her mouth, before Sam hissed back at her.

"Shurrup abaht Lil. It were meant ter be ar Mabel what

were there. 'ow does we explain tharrit weren't?"

"Boggered if I know," Vera replied, "but we needs ter tell Mabel what's 'appened when she wakes up. Them at the factory'll prob'ly think she's dead or summat."

"Aye, an' we needs ter gerrus story right, an' all," Sam reminded her. "If it cums aht that she an' Lil pulled a fast un, she'll lose 'er job."

"Sod 'er job!" Vera exploded. "She could've lost 'er life! An' wharrawe gunner tell Ada Jenkins?"

"Nowt, just yet. We needs ter think this one aht a bit fust. Let's get back in an' put the kettle on. There's obviously no Zeppelins ter worry abaht, anyroad."

CHAPTER TEN

A confusion of corpses

By the time that Dr Plowright had eventually called, on the Monday afternoon, Mabel appeared to be over the more alarming of her symptoms. As Sam grudgingly counted out the coins into the doctor's outstretched hand downstairs in the living room, the latter tried to be as encouraging as he could.

"I've treated dozens of cases of this latest flu," he assured them, "and it looks as if she's safely through the first dangerous period. Keep her warm, let her sleep as much as she can, give her plenty of liquids, and try and get her to eat."

"What's the second dangerous period?" asked Vera, who had been listening carefully.

"If it follows the normal pattern, she'll develop a bad cough. How it goes after that depends upon her general health. I'll ask Nurse Cowan to look in on her in a day or two, and by then we should know how it's going."

By the middle of Tuesday afternoon, Mabel was awake and apparently making good progress. But they knew that there was no way to fool her, and as she sat propped up on the pillows, drinking a cup of hot milk and asking for Lil, Vera broke the news to her as gently as she could.

"But she might not be dead," Mabel suggested as she fought back the tears. "It's a big factory, after all, an' we don't know whereabahts the bang were."

"Aye we do, love," Vera informed her. "It were in terday's paper – the mixin' 'ouse – that's where yer used ter work, ain't it?"

"Aye, right enough. But 'ow could Lil 'ave bin so *stupid*?

Nobody can work three shifts straight; she'd 'ave fallen inter the machine or summat. Oh shit, I 'ope that's not 'ow it 'appened. I'd never forgive misen! It's bad enough as it is."

The tears finally came, and Vera left her to it. An hour later she ventured back upstairs with a boiled egg, some toast and a pot of tea, followed by Sam.

"Sam wants ter talk ter yer, love," Vera said. "But eat yer egg fust, while I pour yer a cuppa."

"It's like this, gel," Sam began, "the factory prob'ly thinks yer dead, 'cos it sez in the papers as there were lots o' bodies what they couldn't put names to."

"Like Lil, yer mean?" Mabel asked, her face beginning to crumple in a warning of renewed tears. Vera took her hand and stroked it, while Sam coughed uneasily.

"Aye, p'rhaps. But that's just mi point. If it cums aht that Lil were pretendin' ter be you, then accordin' ter what she told us, yer'll likely as not lose yer job an' go ter jail."

"Well, I can 'ardly pretend as I'm fuckin' dead, can I, so what d'yer suggest?" She smiled an apology to Vera, who had tutted gently at her choice of language.

"From wharrit said in the paper, it were all confusion after the bang itself," Sam told her. "There was people walkin' abaht injured, an' not knowin' what the 'ell they was doin'. I'm suggestin' yer pretend yer was one o' them."

"That won't be 'ard in the circumstances. But wharrif Lil's only among the injured?"

"She won't be, love," Vera said sympathetically. "Don't get yersen all upset again, but they said that there's just bits o' bodies where the mixin' 'ouse used ter be. Yer'll 'ave ter pretend yer was somewhere else when it 'appened, an' yer just got knocked aht bi the bang, or summat like that."

"Aye, all right, leave it wi' me. Burram needin' a pee right nah, so if Sam could take mi tray, an' if yer could 'elp me dahn ter the privy, Vera, I'd be grateful. I think I'll still be a bit wobbly, like."

"No need fer that, love. There's a pot under the bed, an' anyroad, Sam's finished talkin' nah." She glared at Sam. " 'aven't yer, Sam?"

"Eh? Oh, aye. But get yer thinkin' cap on, gel. You knows the factory best, an' they'll like as not be rahnd 'ere afore much longer."

In fact, they came later that day, in the person of Constable Grindley, who was greatly relieved to discover that, far from being the bringer of bad tidings, he could in fact advise 'them up at the factory' that there was another survivor, sitting wrapped in blankets in an armchair in the family living room.

But of course it didn't end there, and the next visitor, who arrived late on Thursday afternoon, was a more senior police officer drafted in from Nottingham to assist Inspector Cornish of Scotland Yard, who had been given the task of collecting all available information and collating it into the report that had been commissioned by the Home Office. He had travelled up on the night train from London and on his arrival had issued instructions that all the survivors were to be interviewed.

"I'm Sergeant Thomas from the Nottingham Police CID office and I'm just following up what it says in this report I've got from the constable who called round on Tuesday. First things first, you *are* Mabel Fletcher, are you?"

"That's right."

"And you were at work in the Chilwell Shell Factory last Monday night, the first of July?"

"Yes."

"In the mixing house?"

"Yes . . . and no."

"How do you mean, exactly?"

"Well, yeah, I were workin' in room two in the mixin' 'ouse, but then I were sent up ter the office wi' a message."

"What message?"

"I can't remember nah, an' that's the 'onest truth. What

wi' what 'appened, an' all that . . ."

"Perhaps you could just tell me what you do remember."

"Well, it were like this. I were sent wi' this message – it were written dahn, which is why I can't rightly remember wharrit said – an' I were just 'eadin' dahn the main road, towards the office buildin', when there were this big bang, an' I got knocked flat ter the grahnd."

"Can you remember how far up the road you'd got when this happened?"

"I reckon I were abaht level wi' the TNT melt 'ouse. I'm pretty sure I 'adn't gorras far as the other melt 'ouse . . ."

The officer consulted a crude diagram among his papers.

"That would be the ammonium nitrate melt house?"

"Yeah, that's right. I were between the two when there were this 'ere enormous bang, an' then . . ."

"What time was this?"

"No idea, sorry."

"Well, how long had you been on your shift, roughly?"

Mabel thought long and hard, and took a guess. Nobody had told her exactly what time the explosion had happened.

"A couple've 'ars, mebbe. We 'adn't gone on the fust break bi then, I remember that."

Sergeant Thomas's face hardened slightly as he continued.

"And presumably you were wearing your working overalls?"

"Yeah, course I were. No, 'ang on; wait a minute. No, I weren't."

"You sure?"

"Pretty sure, yeah. But then again, I were that confused, after the bang an' that . . ."

"There's a quick way to find out. If you were in your working clothes when it happened, and you just made your own way straight home . . . how did you do that, exactly, by the way?"

"I musta walked. I don't remember catchin' no train."

"You *walked*, all the way from Chilwell?"

"It's only a few miles. Some o' the gels walk it every day, even though we gets train passes; they reckon it's good fer their figures."

"Anyway, to get back to your clothes. Are your working overalls anywhere in the house, do you know?"

Mabel suddenly coughed and sneezed, both at the same time, and Vera came running in from the scullery, where she and Sam had been listening through the partly open door from the living room. She handed Mabel a large white napkin.

" 'ere, love. The doctor said as 'ow yer might start coughin'. It's a sign that yer on the mend at long last."

"Has she got this flu that's going round?" Sergeant Thomas enquired, innocently.

"Yeah, she's 'ad it … er, ever since she came 'ome Monday night."

"And can *you* recall what she was wearing when she came home, Mrs Fletcher?"

"Just 'er ordinary ahtdoor clothes; why?"

"Just curious why she'd have got changed into her outdoor clothes just to deliver a message during her shift, that's all."

He was still ruminating on that telling point when there was a knock on the front door. Vera went to answer it, and came back with Nurse Mary Cowan.

"I can't stay long," she explained, "there's that many dahn wi' this blasted flu business. Where's Mabel, is she upstairs?"

"Nar, she's 'ere, talkin' ter this 'ere p'lice bloke," Vera replied, looking puzzled.

"That's norr'er. That's Lil summat or other; 'ang on, I remember nah, Lil Jenkins."

Mabel had a violent coughing fit, spraying sputum into the napkin, and Mary Cowan looked down at her with concern.

"Well, 'oever yer are, yer not well, that's obvious. But

I were told it were Mabel Fletcher wi' flu, an' this ain't the woman I delivered a few weeks back."

It was Sergeant Thomas's turn to look confused, as he finished taking notes and closed his notebook.

"Something's not quite right here, obviously. You're the local nurse, I take it?" he asked Mary.

"That's right."

"And from what you just said, you delivered a baby here recently, to a woman called Mabel Fletcher?"

"Yeah, that's right."

"And this lady here is *not* Mabel Fletcher, is that what you're saying?"

"That's right. The last time I spoke ter this woman 'ere, she told me she were Lil Jenkins."

"This latest flu, how long does it take before they get to the coughing stage?"

"Abaht a week or so, sometimes less, why?"

He nodded across at Mabel.

"Do you think that this lady could have been working a night shift last Monday?"

"Pretty unlikely, I'd say. Why?"

"Leave it with me; and thank you, nurse, you've been most helpful." Sergeant Thomas rose to his feet and glared back down at Mabel. "Ordinarily, I'd ask you not to go anywhere for the next few days, Miss Whatever Your Name Is, but by the look of you, you won't be in any fit state to leave the house, anyway. You'll no doubt be hearing from us shortly. Now, if you'll excuse me – no, it's OK, I'll let myself out."

The front door slammed shut, and Mabel began to cough blood this time.

"Jesus fuckin' *Christ*!" Sam blasphemed under his breath. "I think we're all up shit creek wi'aht a bleedin' paddle!"

❖

"Well, can you please ask him to phone Dorothy at home as soon as he gets back into the office? It's urgent. Yes, that's right – Dorothy. Thank you."

She replaced the receiver and began pacing up and down the tiny living room, periodically chewing at her fingernails as she waited anxiously for Tim to call back. It had been a difficult enough decision to make as it was, and she just wanted to get it over with.

It had been over a month since they had first discussed it, and Dorothy had kept putting it off. But there would never be a better time; this afternoon was her pupil-free half-day and tomorrow was the annual Inter-School Swimming Carnival, which for Dorothy meant a day off. She was just hoping that she wouldn't weaken and change her mind again, when suddenly the phone rang and, relieved, she raced to the receiver.

"Tim? Oh, thank God for that! No, thank God you phoned back, that's all. Look, are you still willing to come to the churchyard with me? Only, I know it's late in the afternoon and all that, but if I don't get it over with while I've still got the courage, I'll never do it. Yes, now, if that's OK? You're a gem, see you down there in about a quarter of an hour."

She replaced the receiver, and glanced out of her front window. It was early October, but what had been a beautiful autumn day, with the first hint of wood smoke on the wind, was now turning misty, so she took her anorak from the hall cupboard on her way out, prayed for her car to start, praised it when it did, laughed nervously at herself for talking to her car, and headed off towards Attenborough.

The closer she got to the river, the thicker the mist seemed to get, and by the time she reached the church, she needed her lights on. It was still not yet five o'clock, but the churchyard looked, to Dorothy, horribly like the location for one of those zombie films which seemed to be all the rage. She parked her car behind Tim's green MG, locked it, and walked down the path through the churchyard. Her stiletto heels sounded like slow rifle fire as she began to walk around the outside of the church, and she started in sudden fear as a figure loomed out from an open doorway ahead of her.

"You'd make a lousy forward scout," Tim remarked. "I heard you coming all the way from your car. Come in here, out of this damp mist. Someone's left this side door open and I can hear voices from inside, so I reckon there must be a meeting or something going on in there. A good recce point from which to go ghost-spotting."

"You really know how to put a girl at ease," Dorothy commented sarcastically.

"Sorry I wasn't in when you called, by the way. I was in seeing the colonel."

"That's OK. And sorry I was so insistent, but if I don't do it today, I probably never will."

"So, where were you exactly when you saw this ghost girl the last time?"

"Round the front to begin with, then down on the other side of the church, where the memorial is."

"So what makes you think she'll show up on this side?"

"I don't suppose ghosts have reserved parking places."

"Well, while we're waiting, I've got something important to tell you. I won't be going back to Bicester after all."

"That's nice to know," replied Dorothy with an absent-minded air which went with her intense stare over Tim's shoulder through the open doorway.

"I don't exactly have your full attention, do I?" said Tim dejectedly.

"Sorry, Tim, but I thought I saw . . . Oh dear God, there she is!"

Tim whipped round quickly and stared into the swirling mist.

"Can't see a damn thing, to be honest."

"Over there, between the green headstone and that one

with the Celtic cross on the top. Surely you can see her. Please tell me I'm not going crazy!"

"Like I said before, she's your ghost. It is the same girl, I take it?"

"Difficult to tell from this distance, but she's not dressed the same way."

"Better go and see what she has to tell you; it's important that we wrap this up, sooner rather than later. Want me to come with you?"

"No," Dorothy confirmed in a distracted tone as she walked slowly out of the doorway and onto the damp grass between the headstones. As she got closer to the apparition, she wasn't sure if it was the same girl, but then the girl smiled, pulled off some sort of beret and grinned back at her as a shower of blonde curls cascaded down onto the collar of the white shift she was wearing.

"Got ter look mi best fer visitors. An' thanks fer comin' back."

"I need to know who Ernie's father really was," Dorothy said in the firmest tone she could manage.

"O' course yer do, but fust of all, well done wi' what yer've fahnd aht already. Yer've really done well, an' I'm gunner do yer a favour bi not tellin' yer, straight aht, who Ernie's dad were."

"But I thought you wanted me to find him, and tell him about his real father."

"Yeah, I do, an' yer'll do that soon enough. Burrif I tell yer nah, yer might not want ter keep goin', fer reasons I don't wanner tell yer. But yer can soon find aht fer yerself bi askin' yer man back up there ter find aht the name o' the officer what came up ter the factory in August 1917, ter alter the mix in the pahder. 'e were Ernie's dad."

"I've asked Tim to do enough already," Dorothy objected. Lil grinned again.

"An' yer think 'e's doin' it just 'cos 'e wants ter know fer '*isself*? Listen, gel, I knew a lot more abaht men than you ever will, an' let me tell yer tharr'e's only doin' it fer you. Yer reckon that all men ain't ter be trusted? Well, one o' the good things abaht where I am nah is that yer can see straight inter people's 'earts, an' let me tell yer, fust of all that 'e's the best man yer could ever wish for fer yerself, an' that yer gunner lose yer last chance o' bein' 'appy if yer don't give 'im some sign that yer love 'im too. An' don't try ter kid yerself that yer don't, 'cos I can see inter *your* 'eart an' all. Just get back up there an' tell 'im, an' best wishes ter the pair on yer. Just remember wharra said – the officer what cum ter the factory in August 1917 ter change the mix in the pahder what we was workin' wi'. When 'e finds that aht fer yer, yer gunner need 'im even more, so off yer go."

As she faded from sight, Dorothy heard footsteps approaching through the wet grass. She turned, and Tim was standing there.

"I still couldn't see anything, I'm afraid," he admitted. "Did you get what you were after?"

"Yes," she replied, "and in more ways than one. Now, I believe I owe you a kiss, to honour my promise to you in Ilkeston."

As they met, she wrapped her arms tightly round him, and opened her mouth for the most comforting kiss she had ever enjoyed. As he hugged her tighter to him, all the memories came flooding back to her. The feeling of being wrapped safely in strong arms; the sense of belonging; the thought of a future again. And, strangely, after all she had hardened herself against, the familiar but almost forgotten tingling between the legs.

There was a polite cough, and they broke the embrace to turn towards the grey-haired lady with the bemused smile.

"All very touching, but this is hardly the place," Winnie Day advised them. "There's a Junior Fellowship meeting just ending inside the church, and I really don't think this is something they should encounter when they leave. Would you mind going somewhere more appropriate, if you don't mind?"

Tim looked embarrassed, but Dorothy giggled.

"Not a problem," she said, apologetically. As Winnie moved away, shaking her head slightly at the immodesty of people these days – and in the Lord's garden, too – Dorothy smiled up at Tim.

"I have to get some food in first, but you're invited to dinner. Seven o'clock suit you?"

"I can follow you up there, if you like. I finished early at the depot today, as it happens."

"But you'll need to call in there for some wine. And to pack an overnight bag."

CHAPTER ELEVEN
The tangled web we weave

"Well, if Chetwynd's looking for a saboteur, I'm just saying that I think I've found her, that's all."

Inspector Cornish drew long and hard on his pipe, and stared thoughtfully into the distance. Then he looked back at Sergeant Thomas.

"Before we go accusing anyone of anything, remind me again of all the evidence we've got."

It was now Saturday morning, and Thomas had been working almost without a break since Thursday. Back in Nottingham, he had two rapes and a break-in at a butcher's shop to investigate, and he was beginning to doubt whether anyone here really wanted the truth.

"Well for a start," he recapped, "the girl's story's a pile of horse manure. She claims to have been walking in the road between the two melt houses which were almost totally flattened by the blast. We've seen nothing from that area but body bits, yet she says she got up, a bit dazed, and walked – *walked mind you* – all the way back to Long Eaton. Secondly, her timing's way out. She claims that the blast was two hours into the shift, whereas we know it was just over one hour into it."

"She could be mistaken about that – shock does funny things, don't forget," Cornish reminded him.

"Maybe, but it still doesn't explain why she chose to get changed into her outdoor clothes to cross the factory site during her shift. Her overalls were still in what was left of her locker, remember, so there's no doubt about that. Then there's the curious business of this Lillian Jenkins woman. When Constable Grindley went to speak to her mother, she said she hadn't seen her for at least two weeks, and that she ordinarily lived with the Fletchers. When he went back to the Fletchers, they confirmed that much, but simply said that Lillian had left for work – on the *day* shift, mark you – on the Monday, and hadn't come back. And yet when we checked her locker yesterday, we found her handbag, containing papers which left no-one in any doubt that the handbag – and the clothes which were also in the locker – belonged to Lillian. There was an identification disc belonging to her in there as well. So why was that there, when she'd have needed it to clock back in on the Tuesday day shift?"

"So what are you alleging?"

"I've not got the full picture yet, but I think that the women may have exchanged shifts. Constable Grindley – who should be given an official commendation for his efforts, by the way – made further enquiries with this nurse, Mary Cowan, who's insistent that the girl I interviewed in the house is someone called Lil Jenkins. And here's the really interesting bit – Dr Plowright confirms that he treated a Mabel Fletcher for the flu on the Monday *afternoon*, and that there was no way she could have managed to go to work that evening, and yet the clocking-in records clearly show that she clocked in at ten past six, at the start of the night shift."

"Sounds as if Lillian Jenkins and Mabel Fletcher may have been masquerading as each other," suggested Cornish. "But for what purpose? And which one of them is dead, if indeed either of them is?"

"Well, the girl I interviewed is very much alive – the question is, who is she?"

"And how does all this tie in with Chetwynd's saboteur theory?"

"Two possible theories, at this stage. I'm reliably informed that the two women were close friends, and we know that Lillian lived with the Fletchers. As I said, Dr Plowright was adamant that Mabel Fletcher couldn't possibly have worked the night shift, not in the condition she was in. So, theory one is that she worked part of the day shift, then left early because she felt the flu symptoms coming on. But before she left, she did something to the equipment in the mixing house that caused the explosion which she left Lillian Jenkins to face. That ties in with Lillian Jenkins being on site when the blast happened, but this theory goes right down the pan if you believe Dr Plowright, when he was questioned further, and said that Mabel couldn't have made it into work *at all* that day, and certainly not the night shift she was supposed to be on."

"And it also falls flat on its face," added Cornish, "in the face of evidence that Lillian Jenkins worked the day shift that day, and that Mabel Fletcher is recorded as having clocked in for the night shift. No doubt about that, I suppose?"

"Not officially, but remember that Mabel Fletcher has a record for impersonating Lillian Jenkins; we know that much from what Nurse Cowan said. I'm also told that the two women looked a lot like each other after they both cut and dyed their hair. It would have been possible for Mabel Fletcher to have swapped shifts with Lillian Jenkins."

"Possible, but unlikely, according to the medical evidence. Your second theory?"

"Mabel Fletcher posed as Lillian Jenkins on the night shift, did something to the machinery, then ran away before it could explode."

"Even *less* likely, I'd have thought. For one thing, why pose as someone else on the shift you're supposed to be working anyway?"

"To divert suspicion away from herself, of course."

"And how do you explain how she managed to do this while bedridden with the flu?"

"You've got me there, sir. But either way, I think we need to wait until this woman in Long Eaton's recovered from the

flu, then bring her back in for identification and some very
serious questioning."

"We might not have time. My report's due in next
Wednesday. But you're right; whoever that woman in Long
Eaton is, she's got some very interesting questions to answer."

Dorothy stirred drowsily, and turned her head to the right, to
find Tim smiling at her from the other pillow.

"Not bad for someone with arthritis of the hip," he said.

"Not bad for someone with half a leg missing. You've
done this before, haven't you?"

"Depends what you mean. Yes, but not with so much
enthusiasm. Does my performance earn me coffee and toast?"

"Not yet, and it'll probably be cornflakes, rather than
toast."

"I can always nip to the shop down the road for a loaf of
bread."

"No *way* do I want the neighbours to see you leaving this
early in the morning. We have some time to kill before you
leave. Any chance of an encore?"

"The things a man has to do for a slice of toast," he
murmured as he rolled back on top of her.

Almost an hour later, Dorothy took her coffee to the
breakfast table and found an official-looking envelope,
addressed to Tim, lying on a place mat. She looked quizzically
at him.

"Whatever is this? You really are a man of mystery, aren't
you?"

"I'm glad you didn't say hidden talents. Open it and read
it, then I have an important question for you."

"Sounds like the start of a school exam." Dorothy smiled
as she opened the envelope, then looked somewhat puzzled as
she read the letter.

"When did all this happen?" she enquired.

"You remember that lunch in Ilkeston? That was the day I went for the interview."

"But what do you know about fleet management?"

"You mean apart from over twenty years' experience in the Royal Army Ordinance Corps? Moving bakery vans around the Midlands will be a doddle after manoeuvring jeeps and tanks around the world."

"Have you handed in your notice at the depot?"

"That's what I was doing when you phoned yesterday. But, for the record, one doesn't exactly 'hand in one's notice' in the army, one 'resigns one's commission' and I think the colonel was glad to accept it, given the hornets' nest that I've been stirring up in army records lately."

"Will you still be able to look up the Chilwell records for Ernie's father?"

"Of course. I don't actually leave the service until later in the year, which brings me to another point."

"Where will you live when you leave the barracks?"

"Was that *your* question, or did you anticipate mine?"

"Are you suggesting that you live in sin with me?"

"No, I'm suggesting that I live in Bramcote with Mrs Mildmay."

"Is that a proposal or a rental application?"

"Sorry, not very romantic, was I? But I've decided that the prospect of Fanny Cradock's finest on a daily basis is better than the prospect of not seeing you every morning when I wake up."

"You really do need schmaltz lessons, don't you? But Fanny Cradock's finest it is."

"Put that coffee down and take your clothes off."

"You may not have noticed, but this house overlooks the street."

"OK, close the curtains, then take your clothes off."

"I hope this is going to become a habit," she suggested

coyly as she closed the curtains, turned round and shed her dressing gown, revealing her best satin nightdress.

"It doesn't look much like a habit to me, more like a sexy négligée. But take it off anyway."

"You'll still look into Ernie's paternity?" she queried as she lowered herself, naked, down onto the linoleum.

"*Now* who's being unromantic?" he asked, as he dropped his pyjama bottoms and joined her.

There was a crowd of almost a dozen people on the pavement outside the front door as Sergeant Thomas and Constable Grindley rumbled to a halt in the motorised police vehicle. Some of them turned round to gaze at the rare sight, but the majority remained focused on the front door, and their shouts could be heard even before the two officers left their vehicle.

"Bring the murderin' cow aht 'ere *nah!*" screamed one woman.

"They've cum ter gerrer anyroad!" the man beside her commented. He shouted at the two officers. "Mek sure you 'ang the bleedin' bitch as 'igh as she'll go!"

"Out of the way there," Constable Grindley ordered, as the two of them made their way through the crowd to the front door, on which Sergeant Thomas gave three hard knocks. The lace curtain moved to one side to reveal a scared-looking Vera Fletcher peering out, and a moment later the door was unbolted from the inside, and Sam Fletcher opened it a few cautious inches. As he did so, a brick bounced off the front door, narrowly missing him.

"Constable Grindley, find out who did that and arrest them for malicious damage." Sergeant Thomas turned to face the crowd.

"Constable Grindley and I are here on official police business. Disperse to your homes immediately, and if there are any more disturbances, there'll be more arrests."

"Mek sure she gets 'ung, that's all we're askin'," yelled a stout woman without the assistance of any teeth.

"The law will take its course," the sergeant assured them, before turning back to face the front door, which Sam had opened a foot or so wider. "May we come in please, Mr Fletcher?"

"Would yer like a cuppa?" Vera asked the two men, as they perched uncomfortably on the edge of an old threadbare couch that served as the main item of furniture in the tiny front room. "I've just mashed, an' it's no trouble."

"No thank you," the sergeant replied. "We're just here to ask Mabel Fletcher, or whoever was here last Thursday, a few questions."

There was an awkward silence, then Sam spoke.

"Yer'll 'ave ter shout bloody loud then, 'cos she died on Sat'day mornin'. The funeral's on Wednesday, but please don't tell them aht there, 'cos we just wants a quiet do."

"The flu?" enquired Sergeant Thomas.

"Aye, the flu. That's the second in this street already, an' they reckon there's loads more ter cum."

"Yes, it's bad, is this lot," Constable Grindley agreed. "They reckon it's come all the road from Spain, or somewhere like that."

"The lady I spoke to in here on Thursday," the sergeant persevered, "she *was* your daughter, was she?"

"Daughter-in-law," Vera corrected him. "She were married ter ar son, what were killed in France a few weeks back. It's a lousy rotten world, an' that's a fact." She subsided into a flood of tears, and Sam placed a comforting arm around her and lowered her into the only remaining armchair in the room. He stood back up, and looked down at the two police officers.

"Can yer do owt abaht that lot aht there? That old cow Ada Jenkins, 'er as lives rahnd in Phyllis Grove, she's bin

puttin' it arahnd as ar Mabel done away wi' 'er daughter Lil
an' 'id 'er body. They was threatenin' ter break in an' rip up
the floorboards. The landlord'd 'ave a fit if that 'appened, an'
we've gorrenough ter deal wi' at the moment, wi'aht bein'
wi'aht a roof ovver us 'eads."

"I'll make sure that Constable Grindley here goes round
to Mrs Jenkins, and warns her against any more wild rumour-
mongering. And I'm sure he can arrange for the beat constable
to take some extra turns down New Tythe Street. And if you let
him have the funeral details, we can arrange a police presence
for you there as well."

"Yer very kind," Vera mumbled, before blowing her nose
hard on an already sodden handkerchief. "Yer sure yer don't
want a cuppa or summat?"

The constable looked keen on the idea, but the sergeant
thanked Vera again, expressing his condolences for their recent
loss, and the two men departed, issuing a final warning to the
three or four people still out on the pavement.

"Of course you can, Tim," Dorothy said, "I was half expecting
you anyway. But we'll need some more milk; could you
bring some in on your way back home?" she added as an
afterthought, before putting down the phone.

She grinned, and hummed happily to herself as she
opened the fridge in search of something to keep a man's
strength up. Then she had a bath, and searched in her
underwear drawer for something to keep up his enthusiasm,
not that he seemed to require it, if yesterday and this morning
were anything to go by.

He arrived shortly before seven o'clock, carrying a bulky
folder, and wearing a broad smile. She wasn't sure whether it
was one of triumph or anticipation, but he wasted no time in
confirming that the necessary information was in the folder,

and that he now knew who Ernie's real father was.

They decided to eat first, and it turned out to be a wise decision. As they sat, later, side by side at the coffee table, munching on the chocolate mints which Tim had brought in as a celebration, he opened the folder and flicked through the papers. He was like a schoolboy with a new toy as he took her through it, stage by stage.

"It was actually a lot easier than I anticipated. At first I thought I'd hit a brick wall, because there were so many military parties in and out of the factory. But I found one in August of 1917 which seemed to answer the description – one artillery officer, one bombardier and three scientific types. It didn't say *why* they were visiting, but I crosschecked with Chetwynd's memos for the period, and there it was. Good job Jerry didn't get hold of it at the time, since it was very specific about the mixture of explosives, which seems to have been one of Chetwynd's passions. Anyway, here we have it."

He handed over the page, pointing at the detailed entries relating to the identities of those visiting the factory to give instructions on experimental mixtures. Dorothy looked down the list, then went pale and shook her head, as if rejecting what she was reading.

"What is it?" Tim asked. "Another ghost or something?"

Dorothy looked back at him, and her lips were quivering.

"You are staying the night, aren't you?"

"Of course; why?"

"Because, tonight of all nights, I need someone to hold me tight while I cry my eyes out. No *wonder* Lil didn't want to tell me!"

"Case closed, then."

"Not necessarily, sir. I can still go back and check the physical descriptions of the two women. And if you ask me, that young boy on the entrance gate's hiding something."

Inspector Cornish tapped out his pipe bowl into the ashtray, and looked sternly back at the sergeant.

"That was a *statement*, sergeant, not a question. I leave tomorrow on the afternoon train, and my report will be handed in first thing on Wednesday morning."

"But we haven't given Chetwynd his saboteur yet."

"Nor are we going to, sergeant. I was told that discretion was the first priority, followed by public morale. Whatever happened here, if the public are allowed to even suspect that the deaths were caused deliberately by one of the workers inside the factory, can you imagine what it will do for public morale?"

"But what if it's the truth?"

"If you let the truth get in the way of what we are pleased to call a satisfactory outcome, then the political masters who pay our wages will begin to question whether they're getting value for money."

"But I for one believe in getting to the bottom of everything I investigate."

"Which is probably why you're a sergeant, and I'm an inspector. This job is wrapped up as of this afternoon, but I'll be sure to mention how I couldn't have achieved it in the time without your magnificent and unstinting efforts."

"But what about our suspects? They'll get clean away with it!"

"And what suspects would they be, exactly? One of them has died of the flu, and the other hasn't been seen for weeks. For all we know, they buried what was left of her in Attenborough churchyard the other day. I'll conclude my report with the assurance that it was not in the public interest to pursue the matter any further, particularly in view of the likely cost."

"But sir!"

"But *nothing*, sergeant. The same driver who's been

detailed to take me to Nottingham Midland Station tomorrow can no doubt drop you off somewhere. We can start packing now, and still be in the Officers' Mess in time for a drink or two before dinner."

CHAPTER TWELVE

Joining up the dots

The factory was up and running again, after a fashion, within days, but two weeks after Inspector Cornish's report had been handed in, the Royal Engineers were still clearing up the mess. Around the base of the remains of the old boiler house, and across the main road from where the mixing house had once stood, Sapper Hodgins was shovelling debris into the back of the waiting Thornycroft army lorry.

He threw the umpteenth load over his shoulder, and heard a metallic sound as it hit the inside of the tray. He stopped, wiped his brow, and looked over the tailboard at something which was glinting in the mid-morning sun. He was just cleaning the brick dust and mud from it when the NCO appeared from around the front.

"What yer got there, Jack?"

"Dunno exactly. I thought it might be a necklace or sumfin', but it looks more like a sorta disc on a chain."

"Purrit in wi' the rest o' the findin's, else yer'll likely be shot fer lootin'. An' get back on yer shovel – this lot's gotta be cleaned up before we goes on ar fust break."

Sapper Hodgins put it carefully into the cardboard box on the passenger seat of the lorry and thought no more about it. It was too bloody hot for thinking, and orders is orders.

"He has good days and bad days, like all our patients," explained the sister in charge of the Dementia Ward. "But he tends to have a better recall of distant events than things that happened recently. For example," she added with a hint of reproof, "he may not remember that you haven't visited him for a while. Just tell him who you are as soon as you go in."

Dorothy gripped Tim's hand firmly as she pushed open the door and went into Room No. 6. A frail-looking old man sat propped up in a chair, staring into the distance as if trying to remember something. Dorothy noticed that his arms were secured to the chair with straps of some sort, and that a suspicious-looking tube was trailing out from under his dressing gown from the general area of his groin, and led to a plastic bottle suspended from a thin metal frame.

"Hello daddy!" she said as brightly as she could.

"Edith?"

"No, it's the other one, Dorothy, the naughty girl; remember her?"

"She was the black sheep of the family, never lets Sophie come to visit me."

"She doesn't even visit *me*, daddy. She's in her teens now, and has a life of her own to live."

"Who's this? Simon?"

"No, daddy, Simon's married to Edith. I'm Dorothy."

She looked helplessly back at Tim, who stepped forward with a big smile.

"Pleased to meet you, Mr Weston; or do you prefer *Captain* Weston?"

"Are you from Brigade HQ?"

"No, I'm Major Tim Mildmay, army records. I need to get some important information back to brigade regarding those new shells you've been receiving."

"About bloody time; half of them don't go off, you know. And one went off the other day while it was being hauled forward from reserve. Killed two men and all four horses. They're still lying out there, stinking the place out. Damned poor show."

"But you went to Chilwell to fix that problem, didn't you?"

"Where?"

"Chilwell, near Nottingham. Big shell factory, lots of girls filling shells?"

There was the faint hint of a smile as the memories came back to him in still frames.

"Right enough, lots of girls. Some of them are very pretty when you get their overalls off."

"You old devils in arty were always the same when you got home leave, weren't you? Anyone special catch your eye in Chilwell?"

His eyes seemed to glaze over momentarily, then Dorothy caught her breath as he answered.

"Lillian. That was her name, I think. Lovely gel – long blonde hair and one hell of a figure. She was just like all the rest; give 'em a good time and a drop or two of champagne, and they're all yours. Or was it Lucy? Or maybe Lydia?"

"Lillian, daddy. Tell us about Lillian."

"Not telling you; your husband's a solicitor; he might tell brigade command."

Tim shook his head to indicate to Dorothy to leave well alone, then continued.

"Planning to see Lillian again?"

"Not now I'm back on the front. Plenty of others over here, of course. These French girls'll do anything for a loaf of bread or a bar of chocolate."

Dorothy made a disgusted noise under her breath, and Tim took her hand and squeezed.

"Thank you, Captain Weston, you've been most helpful. I'll be sure to let Division know about those dead horses."

"Very good, major." He tried to salute, then looked in confusion at the strap holding down his arm. "Tell Lillian that I'll write to her. And ask Sophie to come and see me."

They were outside before Dorothy finally let the tears

flow. Tim cradled her in his arms and kissed the top of her head.

"Cry all you want to. I know I would. The poor old bugger would've been better off if he'd died in the trenches."

"He wouldn't have had the pleasure of writing *me* off if he had."

"Come on, darling. The huge benefit of seeing the inside of these places is that it makes you appreciate your own life and health all that much more. Let's go and enjoy ourselves. Tell you what, rather than drive all the way back today, why don't we stay the night in Peterborough? The Bull Hotel does wonderful steaks, and we can have a quiet romantic dinner and a good sleep."

"Sounds like a very nice idea," she agreed. "But right now I could murder a brandy and soda."

"Penny for them," he said as they sat at traffic lights in the centre of Cambridge.

"Just thinking how terrified I used to be of him when I was a little girl. And now, to see him sitting strapped to a chair like that, with a bottle connected to his . . ."

"Stop it!" Tim commanded. "You're just getting morbid now. Change of subject. Do you like this car?"

"Of course I do. Is it the one you borrowed to take us to Ollerton?"

"Strictly speaking, no, but it's the same model. The army has lots of these staff cars – except it's got one less now."

"How do you mean? Did you steal it or something?"

"No, I bought it. It's ours now, if you like it. They sell them off through the trade every so often, but we get first option to buy them if we want to. I won't be in the service for much longer so I thought I'd take the opportunity when this one came up for grabs."

"How much did it cost?"

"None of your business, yet. I'll no doubt be answerable to you for my extravagant taste in cars in the future, but right now it's going into the garage alongside the MG. It'll be our first family car."

"You don't have a garage."

"Got you again. But I'll explain that over dinner; we're getting ahead of ourselves. Is that the sign for the A1 up ahead?"

As the waitress poured their second coffee, Tim reached into the pocket of his tweed jacket, then kept his hand there for a moment.

"This is as good a time as any. My first effort at a proposal lacked a certain something, I know, so may I take this opportunity of asking formally for your hand?"

"Why not?" she giggled. "you've had the rest of me." *It must be the brandy*, she told herself. *It ruined your life once, girl, but this time you've got it under control.*

"That sounded about as unromantic as my original proposal," Tim smiled back, "but assuming that somewhere in that crude response was a 'yes', then please accept this as a sort of engagement present." He withdrew his hand from his jacket pocket, and placed a long blue necklace case in front of her. She smiled as she opened it, and then looked somewhat puzzled as she examined the contents.

"Most girls in my situation get rings. What's this?"

"I don't know your ring size, otherwise it would have been a magnificent diamond. But in the meantime, this is a souvenir of the event which brought us together."

"It looks like an old disc of some sort, on a chain. But the chain's almost new, by the look of it."

"Bought two days ago from that jewellers on Beeston High Road. But the disc came from the explosion. We think it was one of the identification discs issued to the staff who worked there."

"It's got a number on it," Dorothy observed, as she turned it over carefully between her fingers. "Do we know whose it was?"

"Afraid not. The personnel records prior to the explosion got shifted south before I realised I might still need them. I didn't want the colonel threatening my balls again if I recalled them, and it would be a bit macabre if we knew, anyway."

"How did you come by it?"

"Honestly, of course. Part of the stuff they're throwing out was once intended as some sort of museum display, then some genius decided that they didn't want anyone inside the main gate without a good military reason, so we finished up with a series of cardboard boxes on a shelf in the stores. When I finally got all the dust off my tunic jacket, I persuaded the colonel that he owed it to me as a souvenir of my distinguished service; I took his derisive snort in reply as a yes, and now it's yours."

"Thank you, darling. I'll wear it always. Now what was that earlier about a garage? I don't have one, so I assume you've bought one of your own."

"And a house to go with it, if you approve of it. I didn't want to jump the gun before I was certain that you really want to marry me, but since you do, I thought it would be a good idea for us to get married where we first met."

"Attenborough? But neither of us live there. Oh, hang on – *now* I get it."

"You're so quick on the uptake. That's one of the reasons I was first attracted to you, that, and your sexy bum, of course. But, as you surmised, I made enquiries about getting married at the church. I was wandering around down there, looking lost, when that sweet grey-haired old lady who caught us snogging between the gravestones came up to me and asked what I wanted. To cut a long story short, ten minutes later I was talking to the vicar inside the vestry, and the upshot of that was that he can marry us in his church if one of us has lived there for a month beforehand."

"So, being the wild, impetuous man that you are, you went and bought a house in Attenborough, I suppose."

"I've not actually bought it yet, but there's nobody interested in it at present other than me, and the estate agent said that houses at that price on Long Lane can take a while to shift, so it's probably ours if we want it."

"I haven't even seen it yet," she pointed out.

"Thought of that, too," he replied with a smirk, as he extracted a sheet of paper from his inside jacket pocket. "The estate agent let me have this picture from his display window."

She goggled at both the house and the price.

"Can we afford this?"

"Do you like it?"

"Love it. But the *price*!"

"I get a massive long-service payout when I leave Chilwell, which takes care of most of it. As for the rest, I'm apparently good for a ten-year mortgage on the salary I'll be getting from my new employers, and they didn't even ask about your income."

"Oh, Tim, I think I'm going to cry! This is all so wonderful! In one magic day I get a formal marriage proposal, a house, a luxury car and a lovely necklace. It's enough to get a girl . . ."

"Weak at the knees?"

"I was going to say moist between the legs. Come on, we've had enough coffee. Upstairs with you, my lad, and in the morning I'll blame it on the brandy."

The precautions they had been obliged to take for Mabel's funeral had depressed Sam and Vera even more. There had been no further information about what had happened to Bert's body, and they'd heard awful stories about mass burials over there in France, but at least they had the consolation of being able to lower Mabel into English soil. But not under her married name, because there was still a lot of lingering suspicion and an undercurrent of suppressed violence in the nearby streets.

Late on the Saturday evening, the local undertaker had removed the body to his funeral parlour in the town. On the day of the funeral, a motorised hearse took the body slowly through the town to the cemetery entrance at the bottom of Lime Grove, where it was met by the small gathering of mourners, who walked behind it to the prepared gravesite. Mabel was laid to rest with her mother and father in the family plot, under her maiden name of Robinson. She had been their only child, and so there was only the Fletcher family present to witness her burial, along with a few of Mabel's childhood friends.

And not even the entire Fletcher family. It had been decided that Ethel was too young for such a solemn occasion, and she was once again staying with Uncle Joe and Aunt Emily. They had also agreed to take young Ernie for the day, and so it was left to Sam and Vera to bow their heads as the local minister prayed for the soul of their dear departed sister, Mabel Robinson. There she would remain, briefly a war widow, and yet another mortality statistic for the Spanish Flu that would linger in the memory for far longer than a tragic woman who had sought only future happiness with her young husband. They consoled themselves with the thought that she was now with Bert, hopefully in heaven.

Dorothy took a long, deep breath, and let the door knocker come down hard three times on the front door of the terraced house in Victoria Street, Eastwood. She reassured herself yet again that this final part of the job was best done without Tim, and she looked down the mean street and tried to imagine what it was like when it was first built, in time to welcome the birth of D H Lawrence a few doors away. She looked back at her dowdy A40, parked near the top of the street, and was just reminding herself of how lucky she had been to meet Tim, when the front door opened.

He looked every day of what must be his fifty-first year, and a bit more. His chin had last seen a razor some days previously, his hair was a tousled mess of grey with a few stubborn black streaks surviving within it, his face was as crumpled as an unmade bed, and he reeked of something cheap and very alcoholic. He stared out at her through watery eyes.

"Mr Ernest Fletcher?" Dorothy asked.

"That's me," he grunted. "Is it abaht that there carncil letter?"

"No, it's about your father."

" 'e's dead, years since."

"Yes, I know. I have some information about him which you may want to hear. May I come in?"

"If yer must, but I can't tell yer nowt abaht mi dad. 'e died in the fust war. Anyroad, cum in."

He led the way through a front room which clearly hadn't been hoovered since vacuum cleaners were invented, and into a back living room which was flavoured whisky and had a frieze of empty beer cans on the floor around the walls.

"I ain't 'ad time ter clean up yet," he muttered as he waved her to a chair by the dining table which looked as if a cat had recently given birth on it.

He's not cleaned this place since he first moved in, Dorothy told herself as she bypassed the chair she had been offered, removed an empty whisky bottle from an armchair, and perched herself as close to the edge of its seat as she could in order to maintain a sitting position while minimising her contact with the actual fabric. She was just congratulating herself on having donned a pair of old jeans when he picked up a whisky bottle from the floor, opened it, and poured some of it into a far from clean-looking glass.

"D'yer fancy a drop?" he asked.

"No thank you, it's a little early in the day for me," she replied graciously. *God help us, it's only ten in the morning,* she reminded herself as she watched his shaking hand try to connect the neck of the bottle with the inside of the glass.

"Yeah, so I'm a bleedin' piss'ead," he admitted. "The carncil already knows that, if this is abaht mi unpaid rent."

"No, it's not about your unpaid rent, and I'm not from the council. Nor am I going to criticise your drinking. I used to be what you call a pisshead myself, once."

"Aye, well I 'ad cause enough," he muttered in self-justification.

"So did I, actually," she fired back. "But I'm not here to talk about your reasons."

"I told the doctor I didn't want no bleedin' psychiatrist. An' I don't wanner stop drinkin', so piss off, whoever you are, an' wharrever yer want."

Dorothy finally lost patience with the pathetic sight in front of her.

"Listen to me, you miserable self-centred apology for a man! You're an alcoholic because you have a very low opinion of yourself, you can't stand the pain of remembering what your life's been, and you dread the prospect of waking up each day and having to live with all that."

He looked up from the glass, and stared at her through a watery haze, partly alcohol and partly tears of self-pity.

"An' 'ow cum yer knows me so well, then?"

"I already told you; I used to be an alcoholic myself. I can help you through it."

"An' why should you care?"

"Because I'm your *sister*, you self-pitying little bugger!"

He stared back at her in disbelief.

"I only ever 'ad one sister, an' she died years since."

"Ethel? She wasn't your sister. And neither am I, strictly speaking; just your half-sister. But Ethel wasn't even that!"

"*Wharris* all this?" he enquired, reaching for the bottle.

"Put that bottle down and bloody well listen to me!" Dorothy bellowed. He did as instructed, and Dorothy felt ashamed of herself.

"Look, have you got any coffee in that kitchen back there? I certainly need one, and it wouldn't do you any harm. I'm sorry that this all got off to a bad start, and I'll make us both one, if that's OK. I don't take milk in mine, so don't be embarrassed if you haven't got any."

"I drink tea miself, but there's coffee in there, I think. I take Carnation Milk in mi tea, an' that's on the drainin' board at the side o' the sink. 'elp yerself. There's biscuits in the cupboard an' all. Two sugars fer me."

A few minutes later, she had found a dining chair without unidentifiable liquid stains on the cushion, and was sitting across the table from him as they sipped their drinks, a plate of McVities Chocolate Digestives between them.

"I really don't know where to start," Dorothy began, "but for the past few weeks I've been researching your family history and I need you to fill in some gaps. You were told that your father was Bert Fletcher, a lance corporal in the Sherwood Foresters, who died in the First World War – correct?"

"Aye, that's what mi granddad said. Mi mother were dead an' all, an' I lived most o' mi early days in an 'ome near Long Eaton; not a real 'ome, just one o' them orphanage things."

"Were you told that your mother's name was Mabel?"

"Aye, summat like that."

"In fact, your *real* mother was called Lillian, or Lil for short. And Bert wasn't your father."

" 'e musta bin, 'cos I inherited 'is cowardice."

"No, Ernie – may I call you Ernie? Thanks. Well, Ernie, the truth is that Bert wasn't a coward at all. And even if he was, he wasn't your father."

"I'm gerrin' lost 'ere. Yer sayin' that Mabel weren't mi mother? Or did she change 'er name ter Lil, or what?"

"I'm sorry, I'm making a mess of all this. Your real mother

was a woman named Lillian Jenkins, and you were sort of adopted by Mabel Fletcher, who registered your birth in her own name, with her husband Bert named as father."

"So I really were a little bastard, like mi Uncle Joe an' granddad used ter call me?"

"Technically, yes. But your father wasn't Bert Fletcher, and he wasn't a rank-and-file soldier. Your real father was an officer, a captain in the Royal Regiment of Artillery, and he was also *my* father. He survived the war, and went on to be a Cambridge professor. He's still alive, but I don't recommend that you look him up. He had a series of strokes, he's in a sort of mental hospital, his brain's going fast, and they reckon he won't last another year. Your real name should have been Weston, like mine was before my marriage."

"Burree never once tried ter find me, an' own up ter wharr'e'd done. 'e were still a coward."

"He never even knew you existed," she explained patiently. "It was one of those wartime flings; there must have been plenty in your war, like there were in mine. Same war, as it happens. I was in the WAAF, and I gather that you were one of the brave young men who flew the Lancasters we used to order around the skies every night."

His hands began shaking violently, and he had been without a drink for almost half an hour. Dorothy diplomatically offered to make him some more tea, and when she came back to the table he had his head down, trying to hide the tears that were splashing onto the plastic tablecloth. On an impulse she reached out and stroked his hair, and he began to cry openly, and blubbered a torrent of unintelligible words. She let him cry it all out, then went back to the other side of the table.

"I'm sorry, Ernie, I didn't get any of that. What were you trying to tell me?"

"It were you goin' on abaht the war what did it. Yer knew that I were thrown aht fer cowardice, just like mi dad?"

"No, your real father wasn't a coward. He was an arrogant,

unfeeling, cruel, overbearing shit, but he wasn't a coward."

For the first time, he managed a chuckle.

"Tell me more abaht 'im."

"Well, like I said, he was a Cambridge professor and he thought he was God's gift to the world. His elder daughter – my sister – was his favourite, and I could never do anything right for him. The irony is that he always wanted a son, and all the time he had one, although he didn't know it. Anyway, in the end I ran away from home, got in with the wrong crowd, had an illegitimate pregnancy which ended in an abortion, married two arseholes and divorced them both, losing a daughter in the process to the adoption system. I've not seen her since she was eight years old. Enough excuses for being a piss artist for five years, I reckon."

"Whisky, like me?"

"No, brandy. I always had cheap tastes."

He spluttered with laughter despite himself, smiled, and reached out to grip her hand.

"It's right nice 'avin' you 'ere to talk to. I don't get many visitors, yer see."

"No wonder," she replied, in what she hoped was a suitable older sister tone of voice. "You should try tidying the place up occasionally."

"Aye, yer right. Ar Ethel used ter do that, but after she died, well . . ."

So that was the last time this place was cleaned, Dorothy concluded. If her memory of what Tim had unearthed was accurate, that would have been at least ten years ago.

"Ethel and you used to work in the same place, I understand?" Dorothy asked, changing the subject from housework, or the lack of it.

"Aye, it were 'er what got me the job at Wilson's. A bakery, it were. I used ter do all the accounts, but then the drink got me again, an' they chucked me aht. I were off the drink most o' the time when I 'ad a job."

"Well, I've got a job for you which definitely requires that you stay off the booze for a considerable length of time, probably until the spring."

"What's that, then?"

"I'm getting married yet again, this time to the right one. My father – *our* father – is in no fit state to give me away, so it falls to brother Ernie to do the honours. We'll cover all your expenses, kit you out in suitable clothes and so on."

"I'm not a bloody charity case yet," he shot back.

"Sorry, I didn't mean it like that. But now that I've found you, I want to help you back on your feet, and don't pretend you don't need a helping hand, because we've both been shit on by the same father."

He smiled again, and Dorothy made a mental note to fix him up with a good dentist.

"It's nice 'avin' a sister again, even if she is a bit bossy."

They continued talking about old times, and as she stood up to leave, they linked hands again. Then, on a mutual impulse, they hugged each other. He also needed a good bath, she told herself, but first things first.

As he waved her goodbye from his front doorstep, she blinked away more tears.

Poor bugger; he had dad for a father and me for a sister – no wonder he hit the bottle, she thought.

CHAPTER THIRTEEN

Full circle

Dorothy smoothed down the back of the skirt of her new beige two-piece and shuffled restlessly on the edge of the sofa as she sat eagerly watching the road outside for the arrival of the bridal car. It was her third wedding day, a day she had never anticipated, and this time she had her immediate family around her.

She smiled across at Ernie as he fiddled nervously with the pin holding the carnation in place on the jacket of his new dark-grey suit, and remembered the first time she'd set eyes on him. What a miraculous transformation, in such a short time. It was only four months or so since he'd waved her into his piss-palace with whisky breath that would have felled a horse. Now he was sober, cleaned up, employed and self-confident, although still understandably anxious about the new responsibility of giving her away.

As usual, it was Tim who really deserved all the credit. He and Ernie had finally met on what had then been neutral territory – the house in Bramcote – and had weighed each other up for a short time, before military camaraderie began to take over. When Tim finally moved into the new house in Attenborough, they had surveyed, with mounting depression, the chosen wallpaper of the old lady who'd lived there, until Ernie had chimed in that he'd be happy to lend a hand in getting it off the walls, since "I've got nowt else ter do wi' mi time anyroad, an' yer've bin that good ter me."

The job had taken several weeks of Tim's accumulated leave, and as the two men worked side by side with buckets of water and scrapers, Tim had explained to Ernie that *lack of moral fibre* was not the same thing as *cowardice*, and that if he – Tim – had been locked, every night, inside a perspex dome on the rear upper fuselage of a Lancaster bomber while Jerry fighters sprayed him with twenty-millimetre cannon fire, *he'd* almost certainly have lost his bottle as well.

"Sorry about the reference to bottle – no pun intended," he'd assured Ernie, who'd simply laughed and offered to make the next round of teas.

That had been a good start, and once Ernie had allowed a Beeston dentist to replace several of his teeth with false ones, Dorothy had felt confident enough to send him to see Karen Meldrum. Karen managed to get Ernie to accept that he was never likely to encounter enemy aircraft fire ever again in his life, and could therefore relax, and had then fixed him up with a colleague who did a nice line in posthypnotic suggestion.

The net result was that Ernie was now totally convinced that any time he tasted whisky in future, he would be back inside his tail-end goldfish bowl, the sole preoccupation of an entire squadron of fully armed ME-109s. Tim had rewarded Ernie's return to the wagon by introducing him to some decent ale, during their regular trips to local public houses in between shifts of wallpaper stripping, not without some reservations on Dorothy's part. As if to confound her lack of faith in hypnosis, she'd never once seen Ernie drunk since their first meeting.

It had also been Tim who'd fixed Ernie up with his first job in years. The wallpaper removal completed, and Tim reincarnated as Fleet Manager of the largest commercial bakery in the North Midlands, he had prevailed upon Ernie to apply for a vacant position as 'Accounts Clerk – Sales' in the same firm. He even wangled himself onto the interviewing panel without disclosing that Ernie was his future brother-in-law, and had steered questions away from the ominous gap in Ernie's employment record.

To begin with, Tim had been Ernie's chauffeur back and

forth between work and the Long Lane house where Ernie had a room of his own. Then, when he had enjoyed a steady income for more continuous weeks than he would once have thought possible, Ernie announced his intention of looking for a car of his own. He had finished up buying Dorothy's A40 from her, and she had been more than happy to drive to work daily in a metallic-brown Singer Vogue which a local car salesman had convinced her was an appropriate conveyance for a senior science teacher like herself.

The final stage in the transformation of Ernest Fletcher from self-pitying pisshead into responsible citizen was perhaps the most amazing. Dorothy had dropped out in general conversation one day that she needed to give at least a month's notice to the estate agent from whom she rented the Bramcote house, and Ernie had asked if she would put in a good word for him so that he could take over the lease. She was now technically a visitor in the house she used to rent, having stuck to convention and, the previous afternoon, slipped out of the Attenborough house where she'd been living with Tim to spend the night with 'family'.

If there had been any further need for proof of just how much Ernie had turned his life around in recent months, it had come the day that they reopened the front door of his former house in Eastwood to collect the few belongings that were worth collecting. A wave of stale alcohol fumes barely disguised the impression that something large and badly diseased had recently died there, and as they recoiled from it Ernie had suggested, "Toss a coin. Do we empty it, or burn the bogger dahn?"

Quite an achievement for a man who had been handed over to a state-run orphanage at the age of five, when his grandmother died and his grandfather washed his hands of him, with the words: *Yer only somebody's little bastard anyroad – yer don't belong in this family no more*. He had never understood why his sister Ethel had been taken in by his Uncle Joe and his wife, while he hadn't, and it wasn't until he was nearing the end of his fifth year at the grammar school that Joe had shown him any interest, turning up at the orphanage and reclaiming him in order to set him up, a year later, as a commercial apprentice in the iron foundry of which he was by then the Works Manager.

The rest, Dorothy and Tim knew anyway. Service in the RAF as the tail gunner on a Lancaster bomber and then invalided out after a total nervous collapse; seven years in a military hospital; reunited with Ethel, who had married a merchant seaman torpedoed by the Germans halfway across the Atlantic in 1942; a few sober years until Ethel died of a heart attack in 1957, and then back on the booze until rescued by a half-sister he didn't even know he had. It was a sad past, but a more hopeful future, and it was the mark of the man's inner strength that he had taken every opportunity that came his way, once sobered up.

Dorothy's thoughts then switched to the rest of her family, and another reunion which had almost given her a heart attack and a brain haemorrhage at the same time. Unknown to her, Tim had made a mental note of her previous married name while they were filling in the marriage application forms – the name she still used – and had also remembered that Dorothy had mentioned living in Ealing when she lost custody of her daughter Sophie. He had then spent a small fortune with a specialist firm of family law solicitors in Nottingham. They, in turn, had made enquiries with the appropriate department of the Greater London Council, which had been lawfully obliged to identify the state-run institution in which Sophie had resided until fairly recently. The solicitors then sent a letter to that institution, requesting that Sophie Younger be contacted at her last known address and asked to get in touch with them for some important news.

Dorothy had been spending her student-free half-days painting doors, doorframes and skirting boards. She had been very proud of the results to date, and the previous evening had gone so far as to claim that she believed that she had the makings of a house painter, only to be brought back down to earth by Tim's comment that 'so did Adolf Hitler, until he acquired ideas above his station'.

The next afternoon, when she heard Tim's car pulling in on his return from work and the front door open, she called out, "I bet Adolf couldn't have shagged you as well as I do." There then followed an unusual silence, broken at last by a female voice she didn't recognise.

"I think you should put that brush down for a minute."

Dorothy turned, and stared at the teenage girl with shoulder-length strawberry blonde hair, dressed like a chorus member from HMS Pinafore, in a ridiculous military-style blue frock coat with gold buttons, set off with a black and white hooped T-shirt and baggy white trousers. The young man beside her was obviously her land-based escort, dressed in army camouflage trousers and a brown anorak.

"Who the hell are you, and why do I need to put this paintbrush down?"

"Because I'm Sophie, and I think you're my mum and you owe me lots of hugs."

A few weeks later, Dorothy still shivered whenever she recalled the shock of hearing those words, the yells and screams, the hugs, the tears, the celebrations and, inevitably, the smug look on Tim's face as he entered the room while she was going hysterical. Mind you, he'd had a tear in his eye, too.

And there Sophie now sat, perched on the window ledge looking out for the wedding car, with Adrian, the father of the baby she was expecting in August, holding her upright with a loving arm wrapped round her. It was perhaps as well that the vicar was not a traditionalist, since four-month pregnant teenage bridesmaids were *not* a regular feature of the Church of England Order of Service for the Solemnisation of Marriage. Nor was the baby bump completely concealed beneath the

full-length floral number Sophie had chosen to wear for her
official bridesmaid's duties. But it was certainly better than
Adrian's choice of black and white pinstripe suit, white shoes
and red open-necked shirt. Then again, that was probably *de
rigueur* for recording engineers like Adrian.

She still couldn't quite see herself as a granny. Nor could
Tim, who had only once called her that, jokingly. Dorothy had
reacted with what was meant to be a pretend knee in the nuts,
but unfortunately it had connected – hard. Tim had doubled
up in agony, with tears welling from his eyes, but began to
recover as she smothered him in kisses and horrified apologies.
As usual, he'd had the last word, advising her that, "if there's
any serious damage down there, we'll both suffer in the long
term."

Darling Tim, always that whacky sense of humour, and
that penchant for practical jokes. She wouldn't be surprised
if the transport he'd arranged turned out to be another of his
pranks, and she shuddered at the prospect of being driven to
her wedding in a bread van.

"The car's here, mum!" Sophie shouted excitedly. "Time
to become an honest woman again."

"I'll turn into a brute of a mother if you say that once
more. Now, are we all ready? OK, Ernie? Got everything,
Sophie? Plenty of tissues, Adrian?"

"Really, mum, stop *fussing*! Just get out there and play
Adolf Hitler to Tim's Eva Braun."

The wedding car was very traditional, and very grand.
The chauffeur insisted on going very slowly through the tight
downhill bends where Town Street became Chilwell Lane,
because of the frost which had turned yesterday's snowfall
into skating rink material, and at first she worried that they
might be late. But that thought dissipated once they cleared
the railway crossing at Attenborough Station, turned into
Church Lane and pulled up outside the church. Dorothy now
saw the familiar churchyard glittering under a thin blanket of

snow, the gravestones softened by what looked like a dusting of icing sugar. But this time, no sign of any ghosts.

Of the wedding service itself, she probably remembered more than Tim, who surprised everyone, himself included, by blubbing silently through the whole thing, using up most of the tissues which an embarrassed Adrian kept feeding to Tim's best man, an old army colleague who later gave Karen Meldrum a night to remember. Adrian had begun the service on the bride's side of the church, but had reluctantly transferred to the row behind the groom when his services as a tissue dispenser took priority.

The reception was held at a *very* upmarket establishment which Tim had selected. As the guests mingled in the lounge while waiting staff brought around trays of drinks, Violet Dunlop silently signalled for Dorothy to join her where she stood alone in a corner, cradling a glass of champagne.

"I've got a message for you from a girl called Lillian. When you came out of the church on Tim's arm, there was a whole crowd of those girls lining the path, dressed in those funny overalls. Lillian walked up to you and placed the most beautiful bouquet of flowers into your hand, and said to thank you from the bottom of her heart. She also said that you had earned your own happiness by being so kind to her. Finally, she said to tell you – and I hope I've got this right – that the disc on the necklace round your neck was Mabel's. Lillian was wearing it on the night of the explosion, but it was Mabel's, and Mabel said she wants you to keep it as a lucky charm. Isn't that nice, dear?"

Dorothy stemmed a tear with her finger, before it could roll down her face and ruin her make-up, and began to thank Violet.

"No need to thank me dear; just wait until I've had a few more champagnes, then introduce me to that cute brother of yours. I see a lovely aura around him, and I'd like him to share it with me."

Dorothy promised to do so later on, and carried on mingling with the guests, most of them school colleagues.

After the meal, it was with some trepidation on Dorothy's part that Ernie, standing in for the bride's father, rose to his feet to make the first speech. But she needn't have worried, and his short, but polished and confident address, in which he thanked Dorothy and Tim for everything they had done for him over the past four months, demonstrated once more the great strides he had made in getting his life back together. And this gave her far more pleasure than the cut-glass decanter he had presented to them as a wedding present.

Tim's best man then delivered the predictable speech full of innuendo, and Dorothy was astonished to see some of those crusty colleagues of hers whom she had written off as stuffed shirts laughing so heartily. Who'd have thought that old Phoebe Glazebrook (Junior Music) would have known the *other* meaning of 'a bit of the other'?

Finally, Tim rose to his feet. He was still sober but there was something in his face which suggested to Dorothy that this was to be no run-of-the-mill wedding speech. But he began traditionally enough.

"It's now my happy duty to propose a toast of thanks to the lovely Sophie. She's only recently come back into our lives, and as you can see she comes with a forty per cent bonus. But in the brief time I've had to get to know her, I've learned that she has all her mother's grace and dignity, as well as her beauty. It must have taken both a great deal of love, and a great deal of courage, for her to interrupt her singing career to come up here and share this day with us, and we thank her for making our day so special. Ladies and gentlemen, please raise your glasses and join me in a toast – to Sophie."

"Sophie," echoed round the room to the clink of champagne flutes. If the guests were then expecting Tim to sit down, they were either delighted or disappointed, as he continued.

"There's one more toast I'd like to make, but first I'd like to explain why we are breaking with tradition by me having the last word. This has, in many ways, been a rather unconventional wedding. You may perhaps have wondered why I chose this particular venue, out here in the wilds of Sandiacre, for the reception, apart, that is, from the lovely meal that we've just enjoyed. I did so because it has a function room – *this* function room – called 'The Phoenix Room'. If you know anything about Ancient Greek mythology, then you'll know that the phoenix was a mythical bird which was able to recreate itself from its own ashes.

"Dorothy and I met in an attempt to discover more information about a tragic event fifty years ago which left plenty of ashes. I'm referring, of course, to the explosion in 1918 at the Chilwell Shell Filling Factory, which used to occupy the site where Chilwell Depot now is. Few of us realise how much we owe to those men and women who worked on a daily basis with the threat of death in order to ensure the freedom of the world in which we all grew up.

"From those ashes arose a new phoenix of a sort, and some of us here today owe our reborn lives to that event. Dorothy found a brother she never knew she had, and a daughter she thought she had lost. Sophie was reunited with her mother, and will soon make her a grandmother. I'll say nothing more about that, because on the only previous occasion when I referred to Dorothy as a grandmother, the retribution was as painful as it was personal. But the most wonderful part of all this, for me, anyway, is that Dorothy and I found each other.

"A significant number of the workers in the shell factory were women, and because the chemicals they worked with turned their exposed skin yellow, they were dubbed the 'Canary Girls'. Last June, Dorothy was – how should I put it – 'contacted' by one of those Canary Girls, who pleaded with her to try and find her lost child. Well, we did find him, and that child, no longer a child, of course, is here with us today

– Ernie, Dorothy's half-brother who gave Dorothy away and spoke so kindly about us both.

"So, if you would, I'd like you to rise one last time and drink another toast. To the Canary Girls and to our very own Canary Child."

Fifty glasses rose in unison, and fifty voices repeated the toast. At the back of the room, on a long table which only Violet Dunlop could see, a group of former Canary Girls, now dressed in what they would no doubt call their party frocks, also raised their glasses.

"God bless yer, Dorothy," said Lillian.

"Well done, gel," added Mabel.

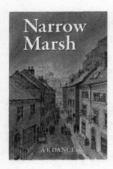

NARROW MARSH
A R DANCE

An exciting historical saga set in Nottingham in the early years of the 19th century

---

Nottingham, 1811 – a time of fear and hardship for the town's framework knitters. With low wages and long working hours, desperate men turn to direct action. And when a man is killed, someone has to pay the ultimate price. Young William Daniels witnesses the public execution, and from that day onwards he develops a burning desire for justice and freedom. But his chance encounter with the headstrong daughter of a wealthy factory owner sets in motion a tumultuous chain of events that will change his life forever. Set in early 19th century Nottingham, in an era of bitter social unrest, *Narrow Marsh* is a dramatic story of life, love and hope.

'One of the best novels I have read. The story just flew through my fingers and I couldn't turn the pages fast enough.'
East Midlands Arts

'A highly evocative story of early 19th century high and low life. At its heart, one of England's most notorious slums. Unputdownable.'
John Brunton, journalist and author

'The sense of overriding hope against unrest and misfortune will stay with you long after you finish this rewarding novel.'
Nottinghamshire Today

Narrow Marsh is published by Arundel Books
ISBN 978-0-9558133-0-6
Available to order from all good book shops,
price £6.99 or **post-free** direct from the publisher.
Also available as a Kindle eBook.

LEEN TIMES
A R DANCE

The dramatic sequel to Narrow Marsh

Having returned to Nottingham from exile in France, William Daniels has now settled in his home town and is developing a successful business as a canal carrier. But ever resourceful, and always looking to the future, he also becomes involved in plans to bring the railway to Nottingham.

Meanwhile, on the other side of the world, one man has not forgotten the past. Residing at his Majesty's pleasure in a penal colony in Van Diemen's Land, an old adversary of William waits patiently for the day when he will become a free man again. And as he waits, he carefully plans his revenge against the one whom he regards as responsible for his downfall.

Nottingham in the 1820s and 1830s, an era of brutal and uncompromising change, and of fierce political upheaval, is the setting for the dramatic sequel to *Narrow Marsh*. A fast-moving story of retribution, radical politics and criminal conspiracies.

'Excellent story-telling. A fascinating marriage of fact and fiction.'
Andy Smart, Nottingham Post

'A thrilling sequel to *Narrow Marsh*, with as many twists and turns as the courts and alleys of 19th century Nottingham. I never knew my ancestors' town had experienced so much turmoil, political chicanery and mob violence.'
Jean Boht, actress

Leen Times is published by Arundel Books
ISBN 978-0-9558133-1-3
Available to order from all good book shops,
price £7.99 or **post-free** direct from the publisher.
Also available as a Kindle eBook.

THE WESTBROOK AFFAIR
A R DANCE

Young Joseph Lambert has enjoyed all the childhood privileges befitting the son of a wealthy Yorkshire squire. But when his widowed father is mysteriously killed in a riding accident, his comfortable world is suddenly torn apart. Joseph's elder brother, the dissolute and self-indulgent Miles, inherits the estate and promptly abandons his young brother, leaving him to fend for himself.

Determined to seek his fortune, the thirteen-year-old orphan makes his way to Sheffield where he secures an apprenticeship in a cutlery factory. Seven years later, now an accomplished and skilled craftsman, he marries Hannah and soon a daughter, Eliza, is born.

But barely is Eliza old enough to know her father, when tragedy strikes. Hannah is struggling to support herself and her daughter, when one day an old lady arrives with an astonishing tale to tell.

And slowly, a forgotten family secret begins to unfold.

Set in Yorkshire and Nottinghamshire in the mid-19th century, The Westbrook Affair is a gripping story of poverty and wealth, betrayal and greed, and ultimately the search for justice and the truth.

The Westbrook Affair is published by Arundel Books
ISBN 978-0-9558133-5-1
Available to order from all good book shops,
price £7.99 or **post-free** direct from the publisher.
Also available as a Kindle eBook.